B. T. Munn

Our Crisis

B. T. Munn

Our Crisis

ISBN/EAN: 9783337378653

Printed in Europe, USA, Canada, Australia, Japan

Cover: Foto ©Andreas Hilbeck / pixelio.de

More available books at **www.hansebooks.com**

OUR CRISIS;

OR,

AN IMPARTIAL EXAMINATION

OF

THE ISSUES NOW BEFORE THE AMERICAN PEOPLE.

BY

B. T. MUNN.

CAMBRIDGE:

PRINTED BY DAKIN AND METCALF.

1866.

PREFACE.

In times of revolution, the passions of men become excited to such a degree that a calm and dispassionate adjustment of difficulties is impossible. The feelings of partisan hatred and resentment are harrowed up to the highest pitch. Both parties seem driven on by madness, frenzy, and despair. The supporters of law and order forget the responsibilities that are intrusted to them; they forget the sacred obligations that devolve upon them, and rush as madly to the conflict as if they had no reason, or judgment, or discrimination. A blind fatality seems to lead them on. They go, they know not wherefore; neither will they stop to inquire. All who do not think as they, and fight as they, are rebels, traitors, and fiends. Their eyes are flushed with hope, their cheeks are pallid with fear, and their limbs are tremulous with rage. They hasten hither and thither, with firm step and clenched fists, denouncing enemies at home and abroad.

The same may be said of the insurgents. No man will be heard that is not for the uncompromising prosecution of the war. War to the last ditch! war to the last man! they cry. Let us bleed and die while we can in a noble cause. Wherefore do we live, if not in freedom, and in the enjoyment of our inalienable rights? Shall it be to live slaves, crushed under the heel of oppression, and ground in the lowest grovels of destitution and beggary? Rather let us die an honorable death, than live a dishonorable life. Let us die as becomes the children of revolutionary sires, who once reddened the soil of our country with blood. Shall we be found unworthy such progenitors? For liberty they fought, and bled, and died; are we not worthy the boon? If unable to acquire, we will die in the attempt. We will show our willingness by trying to acquire our rights; by dying bravely on the ensanguined field. This shall be evidence of the sincerity of our intentions, the holiest and purest that ever animated the human heart.

Such is the language of the brave defenders of every clime. Liberty was the last cry of brave Hungary, crushed beneath the iron hoof of the despotic Cossack. Such was the groan which emanated from sundered Poland, as she was cut limb from limb, joint from joint, and torn and mangled by the cruel ferociousness of her oppressors.

For the reason that the minds of men are so frantic for the acquisition of liberty and independence, and, on the other hand, so mad with fanaticism, hatred and revenge, I shall attempt to give a succinct and impartial advice, uninfluenced by any partisan motives, or pecuniary consideration, on the issues which now agitate and convulse the American world. This will make such counsel more valuable, as it emanates from one truly loyal to his country, and alive to every sentiment which can affect our national glory, or subserve to our general interests. This is what the people need, — something on which they can place explicit reliance. They view with distrust everything partisan, as a production designed for the furtherance of party interests, at the sacrifice of the antagonistic faction. They feel as if they had now gone far enough, and that it is now time to begin to consider about a reconciliation and peace; but how a reconciliation can be best brought about, and how peace can be best maintained, shall be the aim of this treatise to show.

B. T. M.

INDEX.

OUR CRISIS.

CHAPTER I.

"HAS A MAN A RIGHT OVER MAN?"

SEEING that this subject was the cause of our unhappy difference, we will commence with its consideration.

Every man is born sovereign, inalienably free and independent. Notwithstanding this declaration, the framers of our constitution thought fit not to include within the definition of that term the negro. Whether he should or should not be so denominated, I shall not here consider. But I would say, however, as I will perhaps find no better place, that when any people become desirous of rearing themselves into a nation, to occupy, with the other nations of the world, a position which is and has been filled by the rest of the human family, we have no right to interfere; but when no such desire exists, when a people are immersed in barbarism, ignorance, and idolatry, I cannot think it wrong, when every other measure to civilize them and make them members of the great human family fails, to reduce them to subjugation, and teach them the arts of civil and social life, and afterward to set them free. Perhaps it would be a good plan to send them home again to teach their more unfortunate brethren. Their condition cannot surely, by such treatment, be made worse. Let this not be construed into an apology for slavery; it is, on the contrary, right the reverse. Slavery is a great evil; but barbarism, superstition, ignorance, and idolatry are the greatest evils which can infect the world. Civil slavery is emancipation therefrom — it is freedom and happiness.

It is the duty of a civilized people to endeavor to raise their brethren out of the dust, and not to observe a more punctilious but less glorious principle of remaining quiet and see a fallen race wallowing in the lowest grovels of destitution, misery, and sensuality. This does not argue the right to abuse the unfortunate in his tutorship, but rather to require no more of them than will compensate for the expense incurred for transportation, food, and raiment. This they should be willing to liquidate. Thus would we not only be conferring a blessing on them, but it would be acting up to the highest principles of morality and humanity. If all nations and kingdoms and powers should make laws empowering their subjects or citizens to go to Africa buy, steal, or kidnap, any way to get them out of such a place, and bring them home, and make them work sufficient, and perhaps a little more, as an inducement to embark in the enterprise, it should be prescribed, they would be conferring on the negro a lasting blessing which could never be forgotten. It would be the highest indication of their wish to elevate that unfortunate race. To leave them with indifference to their fate is worse than hopeless life-long slavery. But if the inhumanity of civilization is such that they can sit down complacently, and see them practise promiscuous concubinage, infantile murder, cannibalism, and gray-headed decapitation, why, I have nothing to say except to mourn over the depravity of enlightened men, — men who profess such philanthropy that they will not rescue, when it is within their power, from the chains of barbarism. This is slavery the most degrading, and infinitely worse than any other.

As to man's inheriting a right to such property it is too palpable for a moment's consideration. Though they may not be our equals, yet this does not give us a right over them, as nothing gives this except the good of the race. When you have benefited them, you have done them that good; and what is good cannot be made more so; good is good. That children, insolent and arrogant, should presume to claim them as chattels is preposterous. Think of an old negro living under the same paternal roof for forty years, educated in all out-doors affairs, so that he can go on with the work as well as if another was near. The wood is got, a pail of water is fetched, the ashes are removed, the pigs are fed, the cows milked, all is done without his being told; and then to think that a little urchin, who can hardly lisp a word of English, should presume to dictate and order him about is monstrous, and ought not to be tolerated.

Man can claim no inheritance in anything that is conscious, and can reason, converse, and be understood; for the same right could be extended to include every other human being on the globe, and no one would have rights or liberties which another would be bound to respect. Such an order of things could not well subsist; and if any man has rights, every man has. None can claim for himself that which cannot be conceded to another; what one has all must have; for we are born into the world equal. This explodes the European system, those great philanthropists of the negro race. If God or nature had endued one class with prerogatives and powers, privileges and immunities, which another class has not got, then that superiority could be assumed. No such thing can be shown, — still man assumes it; and that very people so rampant in their denunciations of civil slavery, allow themselves to be chained and shackled by a dominant ministry; and still they all cry liberty! liberty! when themselves have it not. They allow themselves to be oppressed, but others cannot be. Let them free themselves before they attempt to free others. Let them taste the sweetness of liberty before they extend the cup to others.

It is impossible for any one to condemn one kind of slavery, without condemning every kind. The slavery in America can not be condemned without condemning that which exists all over the world. If a man has not a right over a negro, a rich man has not a right over a poor man. Still every one makes distinction between persons. He tries to recognize some divine inherent superiority where none exists. Such feelings are not wholly eradicated even from northern abolition minds. They have their slaves or dependants, who flatter every word and listen with rapture to every command. I presume in liberty-loving England you will find that as the lord takes his ride among his extensive

farms, ravished from his poor dependent fellows, he is met at every gate by his smiling vassal, cap in hand; and that same lord who will, perhaps, go to parliament and make an eloquent speech in behalf of the oppressed negro, delights to take a ride in his coach and six, accompanied by his wife and daughter, and point out the repairs he intends to make, at the same time noticing the willing subserviency of his dependents as they totter out of squalid huts, in rags that scarcely conceal their nakedness, to witness the magnificent display of aristocratic usurpation. Slaves ought not to talk of slavery; but let freemen utter the cry. Let those who know its worth extol its merits, not those who are oppressed and down-trammeled. But the time is near when these will shake off this yoke. Soon all the world will be free or it will be all enslaved. Repeatedly has Europe tried to shake off the yoke of bonded despotism, and as often has it been suppressed; the next time it will succeed, and kings and princes and tyrants shall be no more.

CHAPTER II.

HAS MAN THE RIGHT OF JURISDICTION AND DOMINION?

THE right of man over man being denied in the preceding chapter, it must not be conceded in this; for if man has not a right over man, he surely has not an exclusive right to territory and dominion. One is a usurped right and the other a conquered one; both are therefore equal, as it is conceded by the people without the display of any force or persuasion. Against this no one has a right to remonstrate; for the wish of the people is right as far as they themselves are concerned and no further; and this wish should be law respected by all, invaded by none. We will divide this chapter, for convenience, into subjugated provinces and willing states; the former being considered and built up by the power of the sword, the latter as one united together with or by the consent of the people.

First, then, has a power a right to invade another member of its provinces? No. Why? Because in so doing the power making the aggression would do that which it could not wish should be done to itself. One man or power has not a right to inflict that which he is not willing to suffer. And, again, to force a people into obedience is not right, because might is not always right; and because the same right can be extended, if might be sufficient, to every other power and people. Such a right does not select a particular people for subjugation. Because the Romans could not conquer the whole world, it is no argument to say that they had no right; for they had just as much right to conquer Persia, India, and China, as they had to conquer Gaul and Spain. The people of Gaul and Spain had the same rights as those of India and they should have been respected as much.

Because man is subjugated, I suppose it was intended that he should be; but this does not prove it right, that it always should be so. Everything that is, is right. If man can be subjugated he ought to be. Then might is right ? Yes, if he chooses to live under that subjugation; but if he had rather die than live under such vassalage then there is no right or wrong about it. The question is at an end. If my fellow and I have a dispute about a piece of land, and to settle it we come to blows, and one of us is killed, why then there is no question about the right ; the survivor takes possession of the disputed ground. It is right because there is no one with whom to question that right. But if the right be questioned by any one, then it is not right. All opposition must be put down before such a right can be substantiated. When I have vanquished all my opponents, then I can sit down amidst the carcasses and enjoy the fruit of my bravery, and it is right that I occupy it because I do. If any one contests my right let him come on, and I will lay him out as I have the rest. The spot shall be reddened by the blood of the opposition ; and it shall be made rich with their putrefying flesh, but that I shall maintain the integrity of my dominion. So much of earth is mine till I am vanquished by a stronger antagonist. The same a worm might say, with equal propriety and truth. But there is this much about it, that it is not humanity nor politic. It is not human, because it brutalizes the man : man does not fight. He disdains to reason and resorts to the arbitrament of carnal weapons, when either he or his fellow must mingle his dust with the earth. It is impolitic because violent, sanguinary, and rash. All governments have for their end the good and happiness of the people, and all measures that do not conduce to this end are impolitic. War is not a blessing ; it is not for the good and happiness of the people ; it is their curse ; therefore war should never be resorted to. No provocation should be sufficient to disturb the happiness of the people. No judicious and enlightened people will allow themselves to be carried away into a vortex of bloody strife by

trifling wrongs, and those which can be settled peaceably by diplomacy.

Against the right of states to bind themselves together mutually, reciprocally and amicably, thus constituting a great state, no one has a right to remonstrate. The wish of the people is the law. It is the fundamental principle upon which all constitutional, limited governments are based. It is the nucleus around which all equal governments cluster ; all others are tyrannical, imperious and despotic ; these are rapidly dissolving away before the rising light of modern reform. Soon every vestige of them will be swept from earth, and the will of the people shall rule triumphant. The general government has no right to coerce a state that wishes to withdraw from its allegiance, — for the same power that made the contract can unmake it : namely, the wish of the people. Neither has a constituted power the right to bind their successors to the observance of the compact into which they have entered. I care not how perpetual and irrevocable they may decree it ; for a people are not bound by any obligation, human or divine, to obey laws they have not enacted. This would be to preclude the possibility of revolution and reform, which it is impossible to maintain either by reason or force. Our crisis is a case to the point. Suppose North Carolina had not chosen to accede to the terms of the constitution, — and she was a good while deliberating, — could she have been forced by the twelve colonies that did accept it into the union ? Why no ; this would at once have destroyed the very foundation on which the whole superstructure of the constitution was based. All civil, social and religious privileges were conceded by the constitution. Union, liberty, equality was the constitution. And if a state had not the liberty to choose or reject it, it was all a delusion, — a shadow ; there was nothing of it ; there could be nothing in it. North Carolina would have been to the republic a foreign state, because she did not choose to abide by the terms of the contract ; and so our fathers contended. No measures were taken to force her to accept them but they went right on deliberating for the twelve which had delegated them their powers, just as if North Carolina were not in existence. The twelve would not be afraid of her even should she assume a hostile attitude.

Because they entered into a compact that the union should be perpetual is no argument against the right of a state to withdraw whenever she finds that to remain in the compact would be prejudicial to her interests and happiness. A people are not so almighty as to decree what shall hereafter be. They

2

cannot prescribe the conditions on which unborn millions shall live. They cannot take the rights from their children which they asked and fought for themselves. If North Carolina had no right to accept, she has no right to reject; the right to accept was conceded, the right to reject must be; for the people inhabiting that state have the same rights as those who entered into the compact; if not, when and why were they impaired? They have not been; they remain intact; even though they be conquered, their rights are the same; they are connate; they cannot be taken away, no more than you can take the soul from a living embodiment.

If such things were possible there never would have been a revolution, and people would live as they did hundreds of years ago. For this purpose wars are proclaimed; battles are fought; homes laid in ruins; the country devastated; the sick, infirm, and helpless slaughtered; maidens outraged;and mothers murdered in cold barbaric blood, and still the right is contested. People in the plenitude of power believe themselves competent to dictate to anybody and anything. The allied powers said that the Bourbons should sit on the throne of France; the French said they should not, and they do not. Those same powers now proclaim conservatism throughout the European world; they are banded together for the support of that idea; they have won many battles, and conquered many states; but they are not omnipotent nor invincible; and as true as God liveth, they will sooner or later bite the dust. It is useless to maintain such a doctrine, for it can only be upheld by the blood and treasure of the people, and at the sacrifice of the end of all government. The sovereignty resides with the people. This is the old Jeffersonian doctrine, and which has been transmitted through the party of which he was the creator to the present time. It is now warring against aristocratical usurpation; and if they maintain the struggle to the last, they will evince by their patriotism a commendable contempt of life, and a valor and resolution worthy of a more virtuous age; while at the same time they will show themselves not unworthy their revolutionary fathers, in thus choosing to die in the defence of a cherished idea rather than live under the dominion of the enemies of republicanism. Aristocracy and democracy have been the issue since the foundation of our government. It broke out during the first term of Washington; but it was not apprehended that the opposition would lead to any serious result until it began to assume a geographical position. Then the danger became evident and alarming. It was not, however,

thought it would proceed to such lengths as it has. The slavery question was made the issue between them. The parties did not originate from circumstances; but they were a natural result of the existing order of things.

We were organizing our government, and of course an opposition to the measures of the government would be set on foot, not so much to frustrate the designs of that government as to keep alive the embers of partisan warfare, and to check the tendency of the government to absorb into itself all the powers of the state. One party, — the federalist, — was for a constitutional aristocracy, as the basis of the government, with a crown surmounting the brow of a petty slave as the apex. The other was for curtailing, as much as possible, without invalidating their efficacy, the powers of the general government. One wished to rule according to the interests of a dominant, hereditary caste; the other sought to maintain the principle of popular sovereignty in all its branches. One wished to rule for themselves and to modify, as their fortunes might dictate. the fundamental principles of the constitution; and the other wanted to govern according to the wishes of the people and constitutional law.

It will be observed that slavery was not the cause of the lamentable strife now going on in our country, but it was simply an auxiliary. It served as a handle by which to take hold of partisan antagonists. It was a ground on which issue could be taken. The passions could be excited by warm declamations against negro servitude and lordship. Wives and husbands, children and mothers, relations and friends were separated and driven, chained together like cattle, into hopeless servitude. All of which could be exaggerated in glowing partisan colors, in order to excite the imagination and control the judgment. The slavery issue was more a help to the cause of one party, than as springing from any philanthropic desire to meliorate the condition of the slave. They had their own interests to advance. They are more inclined to oppress than emancipate. They care no more for the happiness and welfare of the slave than they do for that of a dog. The slave has nothing in common with them. He will not participate in their triumph nor share in their affluence. They will not allow the slave to marry into their aristocratic blood; neither will they dine with the philanthropist, nor enjoy any of the fruits of victory, or of their emancipation; for, no doubt, they will be allowed to live on the patrimonial estate in huts too fetid for the habitation of swine; to send their children to school, to receive for their services an insignificant consideration, —

one which would be despised by a Broadway poster,—and their food hominy and rice, with the liberty of going with his family to the next plantation, and accept for his labor the same reward, the same food, and a hut as squalid as the other. This is the abolition modification of the constitution. It is a white-wash on the slavery system. The slave looks at himself, his food, his penury, his raiment, and he discovers his condition not changed, — he is a slave still. Wherever he turns, the same doom awaits him, — he is a black man yet. On the whole, I guess they will wish they had never seen their abolition friends ; for they can at best only change masters, and this is a poor consolation.

In discussing the right of states to sovereign power we have wandered a little from the main thread of our narrative. We will now return to examine another important point involved in the issue.

In the exercise of sovereign power might is claimed to be right, because it is and was of course so decreed ; then in the exercise of civil power might is right. It is just as right that black slaves be held in bondage by civil law, as that white ones be held by sovereign power ; and the evil is proportionally greater in the ratio of numerical majority. If the white population is greater than the black, then the evil is greater. But, says the abolitionist, the master has no business over the slave ; the same I have admitted ; neither have you any business over the white man. Must the shackles be knocked off the wrists of the black man to be placed upon those of the white man ? Must new ones be forged for the increase of the slaves ? The slave-holders hold their slaves by the force of the civil power ; now you propose to hold both master and slave in obedience to your will, by the force of the sovereign arm. You say it is not right to hold the negro in servitude, and still you wish to hold the white man in subjection. Now, if any one can distinguish between these two evils he has more subtle powers of discernment than I possess ; for I can see no difference in the moral, whether four million blacks be enslaved, or four million whites, and in our case there are more whites to be enslaved than there are negroes ; therefore the evil is greater in proportion. But, you ask, how are the whites enslaved by being made to relinquish that to which, by your own statement, they have no manner of right ? Simply by being made to do that, by you, which you condemn in them when exacting from others. They have as much right over the negro as you have over them ; and if you have a right over them, they, or others, have a right over you. And this right over you, you will not concede ; there-

fore it cannot be granted to you ; and if you have no right over them, they have none over the negro. But there is no right over either ; still, what is, is right, it it is not contested ; but so long as there remains an opponent it is not. All opposition must be put down, and the people settle down peaceably and contentedly, before it is right ; that is, the people among whom the evil exists. If they are contented to live as they do, it is no one's business to meddle with them. Let every tub stand on its own bottom, and every state and parts thereof sovereign and independent.

If a people invite you to assist them in the struggle for independence, you should grant it with alacrity and good-will. There are no moral scruples against such a step ; nay, it is a virtue to extend a helping hand to one in distress. If one people are about to be swallowed up by the voraciousness, avidity, and ambition of another, rush to them like brothers, resolved to live and die with them in glory, and save them from destruction, or be with them buried in a patriot's grave. There is no exception to this rule. There is no argument that can justify a people in refusing to help a brave nation struggling for independence. The fact that they wish to be sovereign is sufficient in warranting a nation to help them. A blind and indolent inactivity in such cases is the most reprehensible. It accuses a people of ingratitude and indifference ; for there are certain obligations which one man owes to another ; and one is, when he sees his fellow in distress to help him ; if he sees him on the ocean struggling for life in a sinking vessel to go to him and take him on board a safe and navigable one. What would be thought of a man in such circumstances, if, after seeing a signal of distress fluttering out in the breeze at the mast-head, he should sail along indifferent to the prayers of the perishing mariner ? Such an one would be pelted and hooted and burned in effigy, and I do not know but hanged in the streets. But you say the case is not the same of an insurgent state. The latter can have peace and safety by returning to allegiance. So can the mariner by keeping off the ocean, but once embarked thereon his life is staked upon the issue. The insurgents, you say, need not embark ; their life nor liberty nor happiness does not depend on their periling their lives in insurrection. Does not, you say ? A man who would talk like that eighty years ago would have been denounced as a tory. Is the circumstance changed ? Is not that true now which was true then ? What has caused it to be different ?

And again ; a people's liberty and happiness are staked upon the issue. Shall a nation live in trembling subserviency to another's will? Better die ten thousand deaths rather than live obedient slaves. The case of an insurgent nation is exactly the same as a perishing mariner. The one is seeking life, independence, and honor; the other life. What is life without independence and honor? It is a curse; it is worse, it is a stigma upon the majesty of man; and any who can look upon a brave and patriotic people struggling for life, after a signal of distress has been raised and imploring hands lifted to heaven with tearful eyes and supplicating heart for succor in the hour of their distress, and then pass on to the other side, thus leaving them to their fate, should be proscribed, condemned, and shunned. Humanity will show itself human at all times and under all circumstances.

CHAPTER III.

WHY DO WE WAR AGAINST EACH OTHER?

In answer to the question, "Why do we war against each other?" the answer is simple and obvious, "To progress; to establish our liberty and independence." These ends appear to be perfectly legitimate. As to the morality of resisting aggression, serious doubts may arise. Such a theory is practicable when people cease to invade, and when they become fully conscious of the wrong in constraining another. The time, no doubt, is not distant when the people will recognize this truth. It has already found many advocates. I am myself a disciple of this theory. I believe in passive, not active resistance; but until a sufficient number can be induced to believe and act up to this standard of perfection, it is not altogether useless to try to enforce its practical illustration. As far as I am myself concerned, I can carry it out; but I cannot make others do it. I will show by my example; I will teach by precept the usefulness and possibility of adapting in our every day walk of life such a philosophy. But under existing circumstances when there is no other means of advance which can have any effect upon the stubborn wilfulness of the people, it is well, it is our duty to resort to the sword. This will prick up the understanding of the people when everything else is impotent. It is the scourge and the blessing of mankind. It liberates and it frees. It cuts our shackles in twain, and rivets our independence. For us to deny the use of the sword in the progress of nations would be to condemn us to

hopeless and intolerable slavery. It is the only instrument of progress heretofore used. It is the only one that a blind, superstitious, and bigoted people can use. Where reason and argument prove fallacious, the sword is most potent. Where might and matter rules the sword is the arbitrator; but where reason and judgment prevail, the sword will rust. When people will not reason, they must fight; but when they begin to reason, they will begin to have peace.

We will divide this subject into the right of revolution, and the maintenance of governmental authority intact. First, then, if the people had not the right of revolution, and an appeal to the sword in cases of aggression and tyranny, there would be no resort, when the extremity of physical endurance and forbearance is passed, but patiently to submit and linger out the long, weary years of life, till they finally drop into a welcomed, disgraced, and forgotten grave: and this would be the surest sign of a people's unworthiness and incompetency for the possession of so valuable a boon, and slavery would be their rightful inheritance; for a people who do not care to acquire, are unworthy to possess; and if after possession they lose, they are "deservedly made vassal." If they cannot hold, they ought not to have.

To deny a people the right of rising up and throwing off the yoke of oppression when they are enslaved, would be to deny them the right to revolutionize in all cases whatsoever; for it is not for us to judge whether a people merit liberty or not; their own feelings and wishes are sufficient authority. We cannot discriminate so nicely. We cannot feel so sensitively. We cannot tell what others feel, think, and suffer. We cannot fathom their aspirations. Suppose a people have not been oppressed, is it an indication that they never will be? Are they not at liberty to anticipate in prosperous circumstances, what they apprehend under less favorable ones? Are they not at liberty to think, act, feel and govern themselves? To take away such rights, would be to take away that for which our fathers fought. It would be to nullify their patriotism, and say they vainly bled and died.

There is no such thing; man has not that liberty. He cannot undo what he himself has done. His deeds are irrevocable. They cannot be cancelled. He is almighty to do — to accept or reject; but when the decision is made his die is cast, his doom is sealed. He cannot undo, retract, or abolish his work. This is a queer argument, and which no sensible, patriotic, or dispassionate mind will indorse. A man of the highest patriotism and the most commendable integrity would repel such an idea with scorn. Man is almighty as regards himself; he can build up or demolish his own works. He is the architect and the sufferer, and no one else has a right to interfere. He is the sovereign arbiter of himself, unless he chooses to relinquish it into the hands of another; thenceforward he is that other's slave and not himself.

What American would submit to such humiliation? Revolutionary blood would have boiled with rage. Shall their children prove less patriotic, less worthy the precious boon of sovereignty? Dastardly souls may be willing to live in subjection to despotism, but the child and champion of American independence, never. Liberty, independence, and equality are his birthright, and to live in the enjoyment of them is his resolution, or die in their maintenance. Slave he cannot, he will not be. America is the home of liberty, or the grave of the brave. Let her fields be devastated, her hill-sides and blooming valleys and verdant meadows laid waste, yet not a survivor of revolutionary sires will remain to witness her degradation. Let all be animated by such a determination, and the simoom of war will pass harmlessly over our heads. A country with a home is a blessing; but a home without a country, none. Shall America and Americans live in disgrace; their fair fame tarnished; their escutcheon made foul by the blot of servitude? O never! never! never! Let empires, kingdoms, and powers pass away, but let man live in glory, and not a shame, a disgrace to himself.

But, says the conservative, shall not government be government? Shall not the authority of the state be maintained in spite of the insurgent minority? Shall every little town in the country set at defiance constituted authority? The rule of all republics is that the minority shall peaceably submit to the decision of the majority; and this was the agreement into which we entered at the formation of the republic. It was a compact solemnly sworn to by all the members of the confederation, that the union should be perpetual; that the laws should be faithfully executed: that all attempts to resist, invalidate, or make null the decrees of congress and the executive should be put down with exemplary vengeance. Shall this compact, won by the patriotism of martyrs and organized by the wisdom of legislators, be thus wantonly set aside, and its most solemn ordinances revoked by a set of unprincipled demagogues and aspirants who have neither patriotism nor honor? Nay; let the richest, best blood of the land flow; let her treasure be expended; let all her resources be drawn out, in order that the national integrity be maintained and insurrection be put down. In what holier cause can man engage than the upholding of his national integrity, his honor, and the well-being of himself and family? Has he love for neither his wife, children, home, country, himself? Is he devoid of a holy aspiration? Shall the ruthless hand of the insurgent drive him hence from his home, murder his wife, ravish his daughters, and consign his little children to destitution and starvation? The blood of humanity boils at the recital of such outrages, and, provoked, by no aggression, instigated by no act not prompted by the most commendable fraternity.

We had lived seventy-six years in the enjoyment of immunities never before conceded to man. The exile and oppressed of every clime have found a home on our shores, where the remaining days of an anxious life could find repose, contentment, and peace; and where the tender conscience could exercise the holiest functions connate with man; where the toleration of every creed is guaranteed, and the liberty to follow any profession that does not disturb the peace and happiness of society: where the peasant and the prince could alike find justice; where the honest industry in every department of science, art, morals, and philosophy, could receive their reward: where genius was protected and encouraged; where all offices of emolument and trust were open to merit: where honest poverty was rewarded, and dishonest rogues put under heel of justice; where competition was open to every aspirant, without distinction of caste, person, or sex; where monopoly, privilege, and birth were done away. Shall all these immunities be wantonly ravished from us, after having been sanctioned by the approbation and praise of three quarters of a century, by an aristocratical few who wish to raise upon her ruins the despotism of lords and birth without regard to merit? No; let us all, with one accord, die in the defence of such institutions, — the best on which the sun ever shone, or the genius of man ever devised. Let us maintain her integrity to the last; let us not prove ungrateful sons of honored sires, from whom we received their gift as a legacy to be transmitted unimpaired to our successors. Let us not be reproached with having prodigally wasted that, which we were glad to receive, though unable to hold, and, consequently, could not bequeath.

Such might be the declamation of conservative patriotism; and it is not to be wondered at. It is not to be expected that men, in these days of passion, interest, self-love, and pride, would relinquish, without a struggle, the prerogatives which they inherit.

Banded legitimacy fought desperately in the beginning of the nineteenth century for the maintenance of this position. The day of European emancipation has not yet come; but it is beginning to dawn in the West. These can talk of maintaining their rights by the sword, for it is the only way their rights can be maintained. But for democratic republicans to talk so is sheer folly; for democratic institutions cannot be upheld by the sword. The sword is the symbol of tyranny, not of republican equality. Democracy is the sovereign voice of the people; despotism is upheld by the sword. As soon as a democracy resorts to the sword for the coercion of her members, her liberty is at an end, for coercion and democracy are diametrically opposite, — nay, they are antagonistic. And again, to coerce, power must be given; and if we give our power to another, we do not hold it ourselves; consequently, instead of being strengthened by coercion, we are weakened.

Those who think to uphold democratic institutions by the sword are deluding themselves with a fallacious hope. Such an institution cannot be upheld by such means. Instead of arriving at such an end, the reverse will be the consequence. It will loom up unexpectedly before man's astonished vision. He will see his error when it is too late. He cannot retrace his steps, and bitterly will he regret his delusion. That will be no time for tears; they would be uselessly shed.

The wish of the people is the fundamental law of all democracies; and when this is invaded, the constitution passes away. By resorting to arms, you take from beneath the fabric of constitutional liberty the only prop that sustains it. It makes no difference who is the aggressor. Both the insurgents and regularly constituted authority will fall victims to their own short-sightedness. It makes no difference who wins or loses, the result is the same to both the conquerors and the conquered. One is vanquished by force, the other is overwhelmed in its own victory. They are carried away by the success of their own achievements. They become arrogant and disdainful. Adversity makes men; but prosperity makes fanatics.

Very plausible arguments can be adduced on the side of radicalism, but they are all delusive. You may talk of law, order, religion, morals, but they have nothing to do with force, unless it do them all away, and this would be the most likely result — in fact the only one. So those who are anticipating peace, prosperity, union, concord, and love to succeed a state of internal strife, are basking in the sunshine of delusion; for no such happy results can follow the use of such unhappy means. The radicalist says they must and shall be put down at whatever sacrifice of blood and treasure — except his own. But the poor man does not think that in putting them down he is going to down himself. With what resignation could he look upon his brother — his fellow-brother, joint heirs of revolutionary sires, humbled before him? He sees him prostrate in the dust, by whose father's side his own had fought for liberty, independence, and glory. Does he hope to live on amicable terms with his fallen foe — his brother? Yes, we will keep him down with a standing army of five or six hundred thousand men. Such is the language of deluded patriotism! How little in keeping with constitutional liberty, or any other kind of liberty. Does he expect to have his own liberty when he keeps down others by the power of the sword? How will he manage it? Will he hold the sword himself? If so, he will have to manufacture more of them, for there are a great many who think just as he does. They will all have to have a sword. He says he will delegate his power to the president. Yes, and when he gets the insurgents put down and everything all settled with them, he will use the same power against his friends. He will look down upon his poor, weak, deluded followers with contempt for presuming to suppose that he, after having climbed the ladder which they were so deluded to hold, would be held in constraint by their wishes. The sword they gave him to sway over insurgents, he sways with equal facility over themselves. After it is once lost, it can never be regained. The best way to hold power in the hands of the people is not to give it to another; for few, very few, will discharge faithfully so important a trust. Ambition and avarice must not enter into his characteristics. He must be true and faithful, not to party, but to his country. Her interests and glory must be paramount in his soul. No alloy of selfishness must taint his patriotism. He must be as elevated as if he was not himself. Himself and the country must be indissolubly linked together. The country must be personified in himself. He must be the country. For such virtue it will be difficult to find in these days of degeneracy and corruption. Such must be a Washington — and more, he must be great as well as good.

CHAPTER IV.

ARE OUR RESOURCES BETTER DEVELOPED BY WAR THAN PEACE?

Resources are best acquired in peace, but they are brought out and developed by war. In peace we gain our strength, — in war we gain our weakness; for in peace we grow stronger and stronger every day; but in war, weaker and weaker. Just as a family of children are nursed and reared and educated, under the peaceful shades of rural retreat, better than in the turmoil of strife. They gain nerve and courage rapidly. They fear no danger, and they have nothing else to do but grow. They are trained in moral and intellectual science. But bring up a family in the camp, — I care not how much pains are taken with them, they will be boisterous and undutiful children. They will have no refinement nor morals. As it is with a family so it is with a nation. A nation is but a larger collection for a family. What applies to one, will to the other.

A state of peace is above all others to be desired, both in the beginning and in the decline of life. The genius and strategy of the mind can be developed and exercised in tumult and discord, better than in any other state. But who would not prefer to be surrounded in the meridian of life with grateful sons and daughters, all peacefully and quietly settled around, than with the glittering pomp of martial pride? Man watches the bud of infancy in delight. He sees all his children grow up to usefulness in life. He views the opening flower with wonder and praise. He takes pleasure in seeing each married and settled comfortably in life; in short, this is the only reward and consolation for the anxious hours of nocturnal watching over infantile sickness. While the mother's heart throbs with fear, she looks forward to brighter days, in the anticipation, that, should the life, which now hangs trembling upon a thread, be spared, she would see the unconscious infant raised to manhood, to enter into all the social and civil concerns of life, and be a blessing to posterity, and a glory to his mother; she could then with tranquillity and resignation lay down a life devoted so long to the welfare and interests of those whom she has reared.

Thus does every family wish to be allowed peaceably to pursue those social duties so endearing and pleasant. With all the members of the family gathered round the cheering fire; with no anxiety for the safety of husband, father, son, brother or friend; with the assurance that absent ones are safe in the loving care of husband or wife, — we rest in security and contentment that no one is exposed to the vicissitudes of weather or chance. That no one is in sickness or trouble; that no one is lingering out the slowly gliding moments in want of food or water or clothing, with no kind hand to administer remedies, or soothe the fevered brow, or calm the agitation of delirium, — is another source of great consolation. Such happy thoughts are the reflections of a family at peace. The children grow up robust, hale, and hearty. Peace, plenty, and prosperity smile around. All go out and come in with a smile of joy lighting up the countenance. The young man is encouraged to look in such a family for a bride, and the daughter is led to hope for the hand of a promising youth. Her eye sparkles with hope. Her cheeks reflect the gladness of her heart. She is happy. The mother rejoices in thus being able to present to the favored one the hand of her over whom she has watched with so tender regard. She rejoices in the thought of having reared her up to habits of industry, economy, and care. She feels assured that he will never regret having taken her, the object of her love, to be his wife. She, around whom so many hopes cluster, cannot fail to be acceptable to him, seeing that she has surpassed, in promise, the most ardent anticipations. She cannot fail to please him, after she has lived thus long without ever once offending her. This is peace in domestic and social life.

As a family thrives, so will the community, or state, for a family is an integral part of the state, and the state is made up of innumerable family associations. If one family thrives, they all thrive. Their destinies are interwoven with each other by marriage ties and family connections. One cannot wish injury to another without being injured himself. One cannot see another abased without feeling ashamed; so closely is man allied to man. Every part of humanity is a part of himself if he is human.

This should be the care of all governments, to make families happy. Every means should be employed to that end. Nothing should be left untried. This is what government is for; and when this end is not obtained, no one owes that government allegiance; for no one owes to himself hostility and hate. No one is under obligations to maintain himself in trouble. Every one will flee from evil as far as possible, as from a pestilence, and no one can oblige another to stay where the blessings of life and the pursuit of happiness are not protected; where the dearest rights of man are not respected, or where they are endangered or likely to be taken away. He can anticipate any such fears by withdrawing in time to prevent the evil. He need not stay till the malady seize him to be consigned to an untimely grave; he can start immediately.

Man is not bound to continue that intercourse with his fellow-man, which his conscience disapproves; and as man becomes wiser, he will become better. His conscience will grow more tender, and if he cannot adopt that selfish policy which nearly all follow, he can change the institutions under which he lives and form others more in keeping with his ideas. Man is not bound by any law to follow the ordinances of others; but he can adopt them if he chooses. If one feels it repugnant to morals to pursue an aggrandizing course at the sacrifice of the interests of another; if he cannot sue another at law, and take away his substance, without invading the dominion of brotherhood; if he feels that such a course, instead of advancing man in the realm of real worth, abases him, — he has the right and liberty to change it to suit himself, so far only as he is himself concerned. One man, or a set of men, cannot rise up, and command a people to receive his or their doctrine as the very emanation of truth itself; but he can practise it himself; he can conjure others to the adoption of his doctrines. Neither can others enforce their peculiar tenets upon an unwilling people. Because they have the power to enforce obedience does not make it right. I have just as much right to knock down a man who will not receive my ideas, as another power has to enforce theirs by the bayonet. A delegated authority has no more right than a single individual; they may have more power, but power does not make it right, though what is, is. A constituted authority is made up of individuals; each of these individuals possesses rights, but no more than any other. Delegates can be clothed with the authority of the delegators; and this they can exercise; but because they are delegates does not invest them with greater rights than they from whom it was received in their individual capacity. A delegate may have more authority, because in him is centred the authority of others; but this does not clothe him with more right. If I have not a right to knock down another, a hundred cannot delegate to me that right, because I possessed before as much right as any one of them, or all of them; but if they give me authority to act for them, this I can discharge for them, as far as they are themselves concerned, and no farther,—unless indeed, others are willing to receive the ordinances. If I go to work and make them receive the decrees, and they do cordially receive them, then it is right; but if they are forced

to the acceptance against their will, and the will does not change with the acceptance, then it is wrong. Yet that which is, is sometimes right, but this is not; it is only the appearance. They appear to have received the idea, and yet have not.

Civil and political happiness being so closely joined together that it is impossible wholly to disunite them,—the former being those relations and obligations between man and man in his every day walk of life; the latter being our relations and obligations to delegated authority. If we agree and live contented and happy in our civil life, we, of course, would be content to live in the political, and obey the injunctions of constituted authority. If we are not united by civil ties, we cannot be by political ones, except in times of danger when the whole fabric is likely to be overthrown by an invading foreign foe, who, without a shadow of right, but instigated by the sordid motives of avariciousness and ambition, presumes to devastate our fields and meadows and homes because we do not choose to pay tribute, and recognize the right of might.

The happiness of peace is so alluring that many prefer hard conditions on which that peace can be maintained, to turmoil and strife. All the relations and duties of life are discharged with pleasure when we enjoy the pleasing hope that our reward will be great in domestic happiness. Here is the source of all comfort. If we are happy in our family circle, we are, or should be, in all others. Though I must confess that the care and anxiety incident upon the head of a family, in providing the means of subsistence, is anything but pleasant; yet, as things are now organized, this is necessary; if he has the assurance that his wife and children are happy and safe, he can pursue his business with cheerfulness. If he lay aside all his business when he comes in the house, he will enjoy all the sweets of a happy family, if it be happy; and, if it is not, it should be; and every family should be allowed the privilege of making itself happy, as it is the only boon man can enjoy on earth. But this is not the point. When man is willing to relinquish all the happiness of domestic felicity, and plunge into all the horrors of wars, it is demonstrative that he wants something that he has not got, or he wishes to preserve what he has. War is the last resort. Every other means must fail before he will adopt so rigorous an extremity. It embarks a man on a boisterous and tempestuous sea, which, at the best, can only land him on another shore in a shattered condition; and there are ninety-nine chances to one hundred that he will sink. The smiles of fortune are treacherous, very fickle and delusive, and by none to be relied upon. Even should she be propitious, she is then not safe; for all the attendant calamities of war will pursue us at each successive step; and a good deal of moderation and judgment must be exercised, or we will be overwhelmed in arrogance and contempt, which are as bad as the most humiliating defeat. When a people are driven thus far, to stake their all on an issue so precarious, there must be involved the most vital consequences. It shows that they prefer calamities instead of blessings; turmoil, instead of peace; the danger of having their homes taken from them; their wives and children enslaved; their cattle and substance driven off to the support of unhallowed rage, — say nothing of having their husbands, brothers, and sons, butchered upon the battle-field. When a people come to such an extremity, it were wise to stop and consider; it is the result of despair and fanaticism, the effects of which are generally seriously felt.

All the passions to which humanity is heir are then let loose, and man tries to satiate the carnal propensities of his nature. He finds pleasure in perpetrating the most wanton cruelties, and, in some cases, the most unheard-of barbarities. Revenge, slaughter, and blood are his only gratification. Any means that will humble his foe are legitimate; nothing can humble him too low; nothing can exceed the measure of his revenge; all opposition must be put down, and not a single vestige left to proclaim the clemency of the conqueror. It would be a mockery to see a field undevastated, a house not burned, or to see enemies pursuing peaceably the daily avocations of life; none must live who will not recognize themselves as the humble and obedient vassals of the conquerors unless they will admit that to him they owe their all, even life. Base and unworthy the name of man, is that being who can look, without a tear of regret, upon such a state of things. The conqueror is as much to be pitied as the vanquished. Nay, more; for he could have avoided coming to such an extremity, while the other could not. In conquering others, he has conquered himself; in disgracing others, he witnesses his own; for he and that other are brothers, belonging to the same human family. Both, though human, have made themselves inhuman, — the one in conquering, the other in living to witness it. Nothing is more manly than for a man to die in the defence of his liberties; nothing more dastardly than for himself to recognize, by an implied assent, by merely allowing himself to live, the right of one man over another. "What! is life so dear as to be purchased by the price of chains and slavery? Forbid it, almighty God!" Shall man submit to such

disgrace, and purchase peace at the sacrifice of honor, liberty, — all that is near and dear to man? Better had Hungary bled to the last drop, than to live beneath the shadow of despotism. If man has rights worth defending, let him do it; if not, better die than stain humanity with the foulest blot. Better, if every one on earth should bleed, and pass into nonentity, than that masters and slaves should live each in his own degradation. One man cannot witness another's humiliation, without witnessing his own. So, the very moment the South is conquered, the whole American nation is: they have conquered themselves, they are humbled. Their honor, liberty, all, is gone. The shield of their majesty is thrown away; nothing conceals their naked deformity from the gaze and derision of the world.

The conqueror exults. The cannon echoes the gladsome tones throughout the land. The people rejoice, because the enemy is conquered! In another part of the hemisphere, tears of sadness roll down sadder cheeks. The old, the young, and the middle-aged send up prayers to an avenging God for the calamities which have befallen them. The old regret that they have lived so long, the young that they were born so soon. "O death! why didst thou not come in time to hide this degrading scene from me? Oh, why was I ushered into light in time to see my own degradation? Unkind fatality!"

Such will be the language of the old and young. Both will lament the evil which has befallen them; and the conquerors, if they were men, would not rejoice at others' calamity. They would not be glad at the distress of others, but they would sympathize with them, and try to alleviate their sufferings, and not try to make them worse by their making them feel the weight of their vengeance. This is human, — it is brotherly; the other is inhuman and barbarous.

A few evenings since, I heard the distant booming of cannon. It was in Auburn. There the people, delirious with joy, were making merry, with the sounding brass, over the calamities which were befalling their enemies. Little did they think it was the sound of their own disgrace, for is not the humiliation of defeat sufficiently bitter without adding the cup of exultation? How must that cannon sound on the ears of the vanquished? Has not man one drop of sympathy, or one hallowed emotion? Shame to man. My heart bleeds at the thought of such weakness. How would it sound to your ears? Suppose yourself defeated; would the exultation of the conqueror be joy to you? And such calamities are just as likely to befall you as them. Then be wise in time, and not add disgrace to discomfiture; for you may yourself yet drink of the bitter draught which you extend with so much pleasure to your fellow. No man can look with composure and joy upon a fallen antagonist.

In the first place no man will be an antagonist: in the second place, no man can make a distinction between antagonists, though I had rather see a people fight and die honorably, than see them live in subjection to another; an honorable death is preferable to a dishonorable life.

Our sympathies are always with the oppressed: and there would be no oppressed if there were no oppressors; therefore it must always be against the aggressor that we should enlist, not in arms, however, but in the moral of the issue. This, I believe, is the best way to overcome evil, — by passive resistance. This can be resorted to at any time, even after active resistance has failed, and it is the most sure of winning. If the aggressor feels it his duty to oppress by taxing, do not consume what is taxed. No taxes can be enforced if the people are resolved on non-consumption. The articles which we raise we can use. They will support life. Make your fabric, if it is taxed, or go without. Better exhibit a pure exterior than a servile heart. If you are drafted to support despotism, make them carry you; make them fight for you, and, if need be, suffer the ball and chain, rigorous confinement, starvation, and death. There is always a noble despair or a glorious death open before you. Let either be your choice, you will win like a man or die like a hero. Few may suffer, but it could not in any case be extended to such dreadful lengths as resistance by the sword. Every martyr that dies is seed cast in a fruitful soil, which will eventually vegetate, mature, and be harvested in glory.

See the conqueror marching through his vast dominions, receiving the servile adulation of his conquered millions. With what pomp and pride, he receives their flatteries! Which is the most degraded, the king or the serf? But, says one, we must have a government, we must have laws, and they must be obeyed; yes, and you will have them at the sacrifice of honor, of liberty, of everything, if you enforce it by the sword. If every little petty town can jump up and declare itself independent, why, we might as well give up, and say government is all a sham, says the despot, and if legitimate authority ought not to be maintained in one instance, it ought not in another.

This is the truest declaration which a tyrant ever uttered. I will answer it by using pretty near the same words: If legitimate authority ought to be maintained in one instance, it ought in all others, and the case may be extended everywhere. One party has as much right to bring the whole world in subjection to itself, as it has to conquer an acre. God did not deed to a man, nor to a set of men, exclusive dominion and jurisdiction; and one man has as much right as another, and one number of men has as much right as another of equal number. Neither one has rights over the other, whether the number be great or small. Man has no rights only over the dominion which he occupies; and this is very small say two square feet. If I be willing to obey the laws of another, it is all right; but if I do not, he has no shadow of right to make me.

As no good can be the result in going to war, let either or neither win, I would advise never to go to war. It is better that my strength never be exercised, than that I should exercise it to my hurt; and if I do not exercise it to my good, it must be to my hurt. The result of an act must be good, bad, or indifferent, and if I cannot have the first, I would rather not have any.

All admit that man is at liberty to defend himself, and wisdom will suggest to him in what way he can do this the most effectually. If the sword is the only means at our disposal, use it, and this too, with a vengeance. Use it as if you meant to hurt somebody; but if there are other means within our reach which will result more efficaciously, then we ought to use them. To the rude and unlettered savage the sword was and is the most potent, the easiest grasped, the surest to bring about certain results. We will either win gloriously, or lose dishonorably: and it is dishonorable to both the belligerents, — for if one lose, the other must win; one must be disgraced, and the other must be the cause of it; one must feel the pang of affliction, and the other witness it.

The better way is to keep out of war and contentions of every kind; then you will not be humbled nor see the humiliation of others. If I should choose between the two, it would be that I might suffer, for I can suffer better than I can see the agony of others. No man can take delight in, or wish to compass the ruin of others.

War will bring out resources and test the valor of a people, but the issue can never be happy. The strides of genius, the dazzling achievements of valor, strike the vulgar imagination with pleasure and astonishment. It is with pride we view the development of a nation's strength. The mighty armies: the terrible fleets spangling the watery domain; the triumphs by land and water crowning every exertion of American genius and bravery with triumph, we look upon with applause. But an ominous cloud hangs over the scene. Every victory we achieve, every triumph we celebrate, carries mourning and revenge to the hearts of conquered thousands. Many sons and brothers and husbands have been consigned to an untimely grave: submission, exile or death awaits the banished; unhappy thoughts to brood over long wintry nights, while tears moisten our pillows; while at the same time another people are rejoicing at our defeat, making merry over our sorrows and afflictions. A people endued with love for humanity, cannot thus rejoice. No man can be happy while others are miserable. Pity, rather than joy, would be the emotion of a warm and generous heart.

Is it not better that children grow up and settle around the old homestead, beneath the influence of parental love, than that we embark in a contest which can never, in any event, make us happy, but is sure to make all miserable? Why enrage the lion merely to try our strength, from which contest we cannot hope to escape with every limb, if we do with life! Let him sleep peacefully in his lair; but if he comes out and endangers the safety and lives of our children, then let us devise means for his destruction. Let us live in peace as long as we can, and never trouble another. Fight in no case unless invaded; then try every means to lull to sleep the apprehensions of our foe. When everything fails go to work in earnest and drive the intruder from our soil. Overwhelm him with dire confusion and destruction. Teach him that he cannot trespass on the rights of a liberty-loving people with impunity. As soon as he is satisfied that we are a hydra, make peace, and let the tocsin of war be heard no more. As soon as he experiences the full vengeance of our wrath, he will cease to disturb our repose. As we would not be disturbed, so let us not disturb others. Let us do to them as we would wish them to do to us. Respect others' rights and ours will be; but if we wantonly invade others, others can, with the same right, invade us. Let us not do injustice to our institutions. Let us keep alive the principle which actuated our forefathers in the formation of our constitution. Let us not betray the trust confided in us, but let us keep those inherent and inalienable prerogatives which we have received, and which of right belong to every man entire. Let no man ravish them from us; but remember and let us not ravish them from ourselves. Let us not pull down on our heads the house reared by the struggle of patriots, and which is our shield to protect us from a foreign foe, to the ruin of ourselves and the oblivion of American liberty.

Suppose you succeed in putting the rebels down, do you imagine that you have conquered them when opposition is done away? You have then hardly begun. You cannot subdue the mind. It will rankle in the bosoms of their children's children to the third and fourth generation. The work of subduing them will have to be done all the time. "Well," says one, "then we will keep a standing army,— we will keep them down at any cost, — we must and shall have a government." That will not be a government; it will be a tyranny. The Republic has ceased. Monarchy, absolutism, or despotism reign, and these poor deluded fanatics think they will enjoy the sweets of triumph, when they will be no other than vassals, sycophants to the power they have set up. They will be despised by all, — respected by none. They will be looked upon as traitors to their country, and they will seek to hide themselves from the light of day, and the scorn and contempt of their fellows. They will not dare to show their faces to the righteous indignation of offended majesty. They will shrink into their hiding-places like a skunk, afraid of the approach of virtue and innocence.

The party has already erected an aristocracy; but they fear it is not yet strong enough. So they must scatter their bonds with securities into the ranks of the poor. Strange that these should be so easily caught. They are the upholders of democratic institutions. They are the pillars of all social and civil society, and yet they are caught by a golden hook. Oh, what principle is that which undermines the greatest and the noblest work of man earth has yet known, by jewels that only glitter and are valueless. Talk of supporting the government! the constitution! the liberties of the people! Who supports them? Not the administration nor aristocratical domination nor abolition fanaticism. These are the direct subverters of our institutions, of our liberties. The love of the slave is a cloak to conceal their inordinate ambition and unscrupulous avidity. While they proclaim the liberty of the black slave, they are riveting the shackles of white ones. The emancipation of the blacks is their ostensible object; but the establishment of themselves in power is the real aim of all their endeavors. They care nothing for the negro nor their supporters, only that the one may be a cloak to their designs, and that others may hold it till they get it on; then they will turn round and scourge both the negro and the vassal. They who were emancipated are re-enslaved; they who thought themselves such valuable auxiliaries in the attainment of an end are told to keep at a distance; we don't want your help any longer. They who have been so long courted are now despised; whose votes were solicited with such affable words and such smiling countenances. But the work goes on; we know not where it will end, nor what will be the intermediate steps. Time will unravel the mystery.

Some are already trying to persuade themselves that Lincoln is not the head of a party but the represensative chief of a whole people. The case, they think, is the same if he conquers one half by the other half. The triumph of a party is the triumph of a party. Can a country triumph over herself? When parties war against each other, it is the wish of one party to subdue the other. In such triumph the country has nothing to do as an active agent; but she feels the wound most deeply. She is the victim of partisan ambition, and fanatical malice. Parties reek their rage against an antagonist, in the vain hope that only that one will feel the effects of their resentment, while their mother bleeds and dies. Some more scrupulous consciences will contemplate with horror what their own rashness and ignorance perpetrated. They shrink in anguish of spirit from the contemplation of the immolated victim. Her bleeding, mangled remains rise up everywhere before them, to accuse them of ingratitude; for her whom they professed to love they hated, nay, they have killed. As they hated their enemies, so they now hate themselves; as they sought their life, so they seek their own. Life has no pleasures for them.

CHAPTER V.

WHAT IS THE POLICY OF THE ADMINISTRATION?

THE policy of the administration is to build itself up by a military despotism; and any means to accomplish this result are constitutional. Every thing which retards or frustrates this is treasonable. The policy of the administration and that of the government are distinct and independent. Now we will treat of the first, and in another chapter of the second.

The administration are trying to identify themselves with the constitution, in order to mislead the people. It would not answer for them even to attempt what they have already accomplished, at any other time than the present. In short, war is the time when any such thing could be planned with any probability of success. The people have been willing, nay, in some instances glad, to concede powers for the vigorous prosecution of the war, which they would not relinquish under any other circumstances. The people are more tenacious of their privileges in time of peace than in time of war. The safety of all depends upon the issue; in peace the issue is not dangerous; in war it may be fatal, it may not only endanger their liberties, but jeopardize their lives; therefore war is the time for party aggrandizement. It is then necessary to select a faithful and judicious servant in whom to confide so important a trust. It is the most sacred that can be given to a mortal,—the welfare and happiness of the people; and it is one which should be discharged with the most exemplary conscientiousness. Nothing tests in so strong a light the moral worth of an individual as this. If he accepts of a trust he should return it in the same condition; he should lay down authority as he receives it unimpaired. This would be more glorious than the most selfish achievement over faction. When one takes up the power of others, he should devote himself entirely to it, with a perfect oblivion of self. He should forget his own necessities in his care and anxiety of others. Should he do this, posterity would applaud his patriotism and devotion; should he do the reverse, they would execrate his memory with curses. But it is seldom we find one so magnanimous and trustworthy; his own interests must be advanced; he loves power and authority; he is ambitious of fame and greatness; he seeks the dazzling appearances of splendor. In these he confides and hopes to find contentment.

Such is earthly ambition; its influence taints almost every heart. It is felt in every department of life. I would be loth to impute such motives to the chief, and also to the administration itself, if everything did not plainly indicate that they are pursuing a partisan warfare for power. If they do not discharge faithfully the confidence intrusted to them, their names will be covered with infamy, if they do, many will be happily disappointed. Nothing would surprise me more, than to see them voluntarily surrender this power at the next presidential campaign, and give the people an equal and fair election; or make peace, discharge the armies, and go home. But we need not be alarmed; no such blessing will befall us. We have been sold, and they have bought us with their corruption.

This has been brought about by circumstances. Money was wanting to prosecute the war. It is easier to borrow than it is to make, and we were so simple as to stake our all on an issue which might be our ruin. We did not think that that act would bind us to the support of the administration whether our liberties were being sacrificed or not. We did not think anything about our prerogatives. The war absorbed all our attention; and we have been led along step by step, the necessities of the war making us go a little farther, till at last we have got so far we cannot recede without ruin to our fortunes. Our all is embarked in a frail skiff, and steered by hands that look o t only for themselves. We found we had not power enough, so we thought we would embark the class next below us in the voyage, so that if we sank we would not go down alone. There is nothing like having company at such a time. Consequently we passed a law tendering to the poor certain prerogatives; one was that if they would buy a ticket, they might ride with us in the second cabin, and their investment would not be liable to seizure for debt. They might ride and buy up tickets for the whole family, and no one could collect a debt of them, only under certain circumstances. How such acts are to be construed into love for country, it is impossible for some to conceive. We are sorry it is as it is.

Now it is necessary to keep a large army ready, not only for the purpose of keeping down the opposition, but also for keeping up the party. We know not which would rise or fall first, were it not for this farce. The opposition, as soon as they saw themselves not constrained, would rise; and the administration, of itself, would sink into utter insignificance. This is because they rest for their support on the terror of the sword, not on the justice of their cause. A man, or a set of men, conscious of moral worth, will maintain themselves on their own vantage-ground, despising all assistance; but one, conscious of weakness, shrinks from himself to the support of the arm of another; he cannot stand alone; he looks frantically around, if left for a moment; he is racked with alternate hope and fear. The necessities of the case will therefore require force to keep down the disaffected, and force to keep up themselves. The danger is not so much that the insurgents will rise again, as that the friends, those who have stuck to the administration during the war, will rise up and shake off the oppressive burden which their own rashness imposed. Cut off the insurgent States, give them all they ask, so that no fear will come from them; then, let the administration disband their armies, and they would not stand a day. This would not result because they had made peace with the rebels, but because they had not the inherent strength to support themselves. They look upon such an event with the most unpleasant forebodings. They will be sure not to bring it about themselves, and they will interpose every obstacle

to the consummation of such a project. When they get their plans all matured, and the whole power secure in their hands, then they will make peace, not till then. All overtures in that direction now are feints to deceive the people into the belief that nothing on their part shall prevent the close of the war. But should the insurgents concede all that is now required of them, a new obstacle would be presented by another dishonorable demand; and, should this be granted, another and another will be presented. Nothing could induce them to make peace at this juncture.

Every pretext will be sought to keep the war-spirit up, and keep the army on foot. When they show no reason for sustaining an army, pretexts will not be wanting to sustain it elsewhere. The policy of this party has always been against France, and in favor of England. Jacobin absolutism is inimical to aristocratical usurpation; and with the English aristocracy they have always manifested a deep sympathy; consequently, it will be war with France, and peace with England. This is a serious accusation; but it is one which can be sufficiently substantiated by historical documents. In the war of 1812, the federalists — and they are in power now — sought every means to weaken the hands of the administration, and prevent the successful termination of the war. Every measure introduced into Congress for a vigorous prosecution of the war was obstinately opposed by nearly every federal member. Then the parties had not assumed their present geographical position. All New England was, at times, the most bitter opponent of the federal parties; now they are its most faithful supporters. They were the opponents of the protective system, and the South were its supporters.

The foreign sympathies of the parties are the most important. Our internal concerns will take care of themselves, if we take care of our foreign matters, just as dollars will take care of themselves if we take care of the cents. We can trace the hostility of the federalists to France and friendship for England to the very commencement of our political existence. In the convention which assembled to frame the constitution and organize the government, it showed itself to a remarkable extent. The federalists were for concentrating into the hands of the general government all the powers of the State; while the republicans, now the democrats, were for limiting the powers of the legislature and executive — without, however, making them powerless — as much as possible. They wanted to hold the power in their own hands, and dole it out, in cases of necessity, to the administration; while the former wished to make it absolute, so as to be able to *com-*

pel recusant States to do what they thought was their duty. This is nothing less than constitutional aristocracy, such as that with which England is now blessed ; and this is observable through the whole period of our national existence. The republicans did, once or twice, compelled by the clamors of the people, create a national bank : but it was oftener vetoed, sometimes lost in the houses. Nothing is more subversive of democratic institutions than an organized bank system. It corrupts the public functionaries, and identifies the money-class with the administration, which, as we now experience, to our cost, destroys the influence of the popular voice, because the popular voice is never in sympathy with the wealthy. One is always trying to rise in the world, and the other is trying to keep him down. One wishes to keep himself rich, and, to do this, he must keep the other poor : for every one cannot be rich, and, the richer the rich are, the poorer the poor are. For an illustration of this, look at England. There, some own yearly incomes to the amount of $100 to $250,000, while others toil along from hand to mouth, in want of bread and clothes. If living examples are not sufficient, we can prove it theoretically. For instance: how can one end of a string exist without the other ? Who was poor fifty years ago ? A few, very few, were perhaps rich ; but no one was called poor who had his health, was industrious and brave. No one was extremely poor, because many were not extremely rich. But now, as more have grown rich, many have grown poor in the same ratio; and as the rich grow richer, the poor grow poorer. If one extreme exists, the other must; but, if neither does, we occupy the mean. Therefore, if the poor wish to be ground down as low as England's poor are, let them support the rich in their assumption of aristocratical majesty ; but if they wish to enjoy the position of human beings, let them tear down this party, and place themselves at the head of the government. They must either rule or suffer ; there is no other alternative. We have got to be democratic or aristocratic. Choose ye this day whom ye will serve, your country and democracy, or aristocracy and faction. It may not be too late to restore the democracy on a modified platform, by promising to recognize the existing indebtedness; for what has been contracted in good faith by many who did not know the result of such an act, and are therefore guiltless of any intentional wrong, should be promptly met and faithfully paid.

The administration then are naturally inclined to a war with France. A pretext is not wanting. Bordering on the American States is a power too ignorant to govern themselves and too proud to be governed. They have changed this government since 1821 many times. In this country, contrary to the Monroe doctrine, France has obtained a nominal foothold. She has given Mexico a king, who must be upheld by foreign bayonets, else he would sink into the marsh. The question now is whether there is danger to be apprehended from this quarter. Can Maximilian make the people of Mexico French ? They to us are foreigners, but not French. If France herself were there, there would be danger ; but as it is, no apprehension need be entertained. Let them alone, and they will soon drive him out. They cannot stay long under any government, even if it be their own erecting. And another thing : what can we do with him ? Suppose we go to war with them and drive him out ; what then ? Will he stay out ? What will hinder him from coming again and usurping the sovereignty as soon as our backs are turned and we engaged in some other business of more importance than the whole Mexican nation ? Or must we keep a hundred thousand men in arms in order to keep a people in obedience to law who cannot keep themselves so ? They do not wish our interference; neither would they thank us for our trouble. Suppose we take them into the Union ; they can neither speak our language nor we theirs. They would be nothing but a bill of expense to us. They are an annoyance to themselves. They can neither appreciate nor return a favor. They are a mixed, heterogeneous nation, half barbarous, bigoted, and superstitious. Let us not meddle with a people who will neither repay us, nor be blessed with our pains. They would neither prove useful to us nor to themselves. This time has already proved. If they were oppressed and struggling for freedom, and would improve it when they had it, why, I should be the first for succoring them; but while they are satisfied with their lot, let them alone, especially as they neither have the power nor the inclination to trouble us. If the French can make anything of them, let them : it will only prepare them for a better appreciation of the liberties which we enjoy, and which we would not be loth to extend to them; as soon as they are able to feel such a gift a favor, we will give it to them. The French can never make them a French nation, if they were allowed the peaceable possession of the throne, nor breathe into their effeminate souls a brave spirit. They are what they are, and no government, with the means at their disposal, can make them otherwise. Being then what they are, they can be of no possible danger to us, and of no possible advantage to any one. They are a people whose interests, passions and sympathies are distinct from ours. Their genius is peculiar to themselves, with which no other can amalgamate. They have tried to govern themselves without success. Let them live and learn, and be prepared for better times. None would view with more delight than myself the annexation of the Mexican nation, and it may sometime take place; but it would be the greatest calamity that could befall us if it should now take place. Let them be tutored beneath the chastening rod of affliction, and they will know something. Then they will appreciate a liberation therefrom, and be prepared to enter the Union.

This, then, will be no good excuse for keeping up the armies; for where there is nothing to be gained, there may be danger of losing all. Let us not risk so precious an inheritance for one so mean. If they are conquered, they win a glorious victory; if we be conquered, we lose our all. The risks are not proportionate; neither would a victory over them pay the expense; we have everything to lose and nothing to gain in any event.

Some apprehend that the South will ally itself with Mexico. There is no danger of any such thing, even should France give her assent; for there is no common sympathy between the two. Of course they are near, and it would be easy to unite them if their genius was adapted. The British possessions border on the Polar regions, but they do not apprehend any danger of an alliance between their colonies and the Esquimaux, nor invasion from the Esquimaux. The danger on the other side of us is equally as real. It is only imaginary in either case, neither would it add to the glory of our arms to vanquish the whole of them; for in that case we could make no distinction between civil and foreign enemies. As long as the South struggle bravely alone, they will have the sympathy of every patriot, and every true lover of liberty. They are aware of this, and I will warrant that they will never weaken their cause by calling in a foreign foe which can only call discomfiture to their arms.

The policy of the administration on the start would have been to give the South assurances that they would be protected in their rights and privileges, and there would have been no war. But this was not what the administration wanted, — they wanted war; for in war they could effect the designs they had against slavery, and could reek their vengeance against a political enemy better than in peace. They would not even recognize their commissioners who came to get such assurances, because in so doing they would tacitly admit that they were an inde-

pendent nation; but they must make peace with them sometime, and then they will recognize them as such any way. So you see that they adopted a very puerile excuse for not negotiating with them then, and one which will not bear, in order to justify them, the least examination. That they did wrong in thus plunging the country into all the horrors of civil war, no one will deny. That they would have conferred on the country the greatest blessings she could enjoy, and on themselves imperishable and honorable renown by receiving them with gladness, and conceding them all they might deem it for their safety to request, no one will deny except the deluded fanatic. That they could have done this without derogating from the majesty of the Republic every one will maintain. What they would have asked, we can only conjecture; but they could have asked for nothing but what could have been conceded; and what could have been conceded, ought to have been, — for everything should be done before a nation plunges rashly into war. But everything the administration refused to do.

The administration think they are obliged by their oath to bring back into the Union all recusant members. The oath directed them to maintain the integrity of the Union entire, or, if you please, of the United States. Now, what constitutes the United States? All those that choose to remain in the Union, and abide by the terms of the contract. Yes, this is the Union. We have seen that the wish of the people is the law. They have the right to make contracts, and to unmake them. Consequently, the Union consists of such and such States only that choose to be so considered. The people of a territory cannot, by right, nor by the terms of the constitution, be forced into the Union; and if a territory has the right to choose for itself, has not a State, or does a State, by becoming such lose all her rights? This is a strange doctrine, and it is one which is not admissible by a Republican people.

Then they were in possession of all the forts, arsenals, magazines, and public works and buildings of all kinds, at the time of their accession. Certainly. The Union consisted of all those States which adhered to the terms of the compact. Territories and States that had withdrawn their allegiance, stood exactly upon the same footing. The territories and states had rights, and they had the right to exercise those rights. If States have no rights, man has none. neither here nor there ; so those who maintain that States have no rights after their acceptance of the Constitution, are only taking from themselves those inherent and inalienable prerogatives which are the pride and glory of the American name.

Suppose they had all withdrawn themselves but Maryland and Virginia, there would still have been a Union, and it would have extended no further than the limits of those States; and if they had taken an oath, on their assumption of the sovereignty, to maintain the property of the Union, they would have been under obligation to faithfully discharge the duties which they thus took upon themselves; neither would there be a departure from the letter of that oath if they only maintained the property of those two States. Those were the only States in the Union. They might just as well maintain that their oath obliged them to go to Brazil and conquer that State, as to maintain that it obliged them to conquer South Carolina. They stand upon an equal footing as respects the Union. One they could conquer just as legitimately as the other. They had just as much right over Brazil as over South Carolina. Such doctrines democrats must maintain, else they will be maintained by none. Neither aristocracies, nor oligarchies, nor monarchies will maintain them, I will assure you.

From the first establishment of the American Republic a latent tendency toward aristocracy can be discovered in the federal party; and this party, as we before observed, is now represented by the republican or abolition party. They are ready to ally themselves to any and every power which has any sympathy with their own pretensions. It is their wish to build up just such an institution as now exists in England. They would reduce the States to mere provinces, shorn of all power, dignity and regard, thereby concentrating into themselves all the resources of the American State. They would bring the people into subserviency to their will, making them vassals of absolutism. The sooner the people discover this truth, the easier will it be for them to check the designs of the administration against their liberties, and finally to subvert all their plans of selfish aggrandisement. Should the people rise as one man and proclaim the integrity of American institutions, all the evils resulting from a concentration of power in the hands of a few would be avoided; but we cannot hope for anything so good, and one which would prove so beneficial to the people. When a people begin to decline, they go with such vengeance that no finite power can stay them. Nothing short of a miraculous interposition of Providence can help us; for the way to destruction is easy and gentle, but the way to salvation is difficult and hard.

This is why so many sympathized with England during the war of 1812; and there was no one, but those who favored the views of the present administration, that were opposed to it; and these were opposed to it only because they sympathized with England's aristocracy. They did not wish to war against what they sought to establish. English institutions they loved, and they were endeavoring to transplant them on American soil. For this end they have labored during the whole existence of our democracy; and now, with the power in their hands, they will accomplish much. They will not fight against England, nor English institutions. It matters not what the provocation may be, it will never be sufficient, in their minds, to take up arms. The national honor may be insulted with impunity, as it was in the case of the Chesapeake, and they will be its apologists. They are allied together in sympathy and interest, and anything that each may do will be applauded by the other. The cause of one is the cause of both. They will stand or fall together. So long as England maintains herself in present power, so long she will find a faithful friend and ally in the present administration, or those who support it.

Should the Canadian Provinces revolt and appeal to young America for help, I have not the least scruple in affirming that the administration would be inclined, if it did not really help to put down the insurgents. Abundant pretences will be adduced to show the necessity of a war with France, and at the same time peace with England. Some excuse will be sought for keeping the army on foot; but it will not be for the emancipation of the Canadian Provinces. They may struggle and die within sight and hearing of American liberty; still stringent orders will be enforced for the suppression of every attempt tending to help the bleeding patriots. However much the people may wish to be avenged on the haughty mistress of the ocean, still they will not be allowed to humble again that proud foe, by the masters they themselves have set up. The groans of thousands may come on the midnight air across the stream which divides constitutional liberty from usurped despotism; but they will fall on ears deaf to that martial sound. We who once so gloriously fought, bled, and conquered for that same inestimable boon, and against the same foe, prove ourselves ingrates to the memory of our fathers, by not cherishing the same patriotic love for liberty and independence for which they fought, and the same unconquerable animosity against their foe. We, by loving their enemies, and aiding them by our sympathy and countenance, say that their love of liberty was false, and their patriotism selfish. They fought for liberty and independence, and these we are wantonly throwing away, by refusing to aid others in the attainment of like privileges and immunities.

We sought aid of a foreign friend and obtained it; they will seek it of a neighbor and not get it, and of her who of all others should be the last to refuse it. We would have thought it hard could we not have obtained the succor which carried us triumphantly through our struggle. What will the Canadians think when they come to us as we went to the French and ask us for that which we were not ashamed then to solicit, and this too against the same foe? What answer shall we return? How shall we look and act in the presence of patriots? We who received, and proved ourselves unable to hold the dearest blessings ever transmitted to posterity. It remains for us to prevent the adjustment of such a yoke. We should strive to retain possession of ourselves so that we may act as our consciences may dictate, and not tremble in subserviency to a power hostile to our interests, and inimical to our institutions. Such is the policy of the administration. We will now show what is the policy of the government.

CHAPTER VI.

THE POLICY OF THE ADMINISTRATION.

The policy of our government is to keep alive the spirit of our ancient institutions. The rights and sovereignty of states should be respected. Peace and amity should reign among us. Every political difference should be settled by conciliation on the part of one, and peaceful acquiescence to just and reasonable terms on the part of the other. Every partisan consideration should be sacrificed for the purpose of maintaining peace among ourselves; and this is the only way that republican institutions can be sustained. If you go to war on a political issue, and subjugate a state, the republic is at an end; for the very name of a republic is synonymous of individual and state sovereignty; if states have no rights, individuals have none; and in democracies the popular voice is the law of the land. The popular voice is democratic — it is the prop of our institutions, take it away and the whole falls to the ground.

But how, it may be asked, can popular institutions be maintained entire? One portion of the state may be an agricultural district; another a manufacturing district. It may be for the manufacturing interest to have a protective tariff, and it may be for the agricultural interests to have none, or, at least a very small tariff. How are these interests to be reconciled? If regulations did not interfere it could be so arranged that an agricultural portion of a state need not beggar itself to enrich another portion. It is not right that a part of a whole starve itself, to feed another to surfeity. A tariff is for the protection of a state against foreign competition, and not that one portion of a state may enrich itself at the expense of another. If regulations prevent the judicious adjustment of such issues, they should be modified or repealed. The end of a protective system is attained when foreigners are prevented from introducing their fabrics; it is not designed to protect one portion of a state and impoverish another; therefore such articles as are manufactured and are required by a state should be left free, or nearly so, of duty at ports within the state; but let foreign commodities be excluded by a rigorous tariff. Duties should be uniform throughout a state, so that one portion of the people will not pay more for certain articles than another; neither should foreign powers be allowed to come in with as good an article, and undersell us because of their cheaper labor. Such conflicting interests can some way or another be reconciled without proceeding to extremities. If the constitution conflicts, change it. No people have a right to prescribe conditions on which future generations shall associate, nor on what terms they shall trade. The same right that one people assumes, should, and must be conceded to another — that of legislating for themselves. How can one generation anticipate the wants and necessities of another. Such presumption on the part of another should be repelled; any one may advise, but let no one command.

The constitutional objections which many have made to salutary and beneficial laws are puerile; and these objections are oftener dictated by policy than by any intrinsic unusefulness. Measures have from time to time been recommended to Congress, which were very necessary for the further development of our resources, against which, though many might think them needful, the hue-and-cry would be raised, UNCONSTITUTIONAL! The spirit of opposition seems to be connatural with Democracy. This is right enough, as far as I know; but it need not shelter itself under such a mask. Let not demagoguism be concealed under pretended devotion to country. If a measure be objectionable, oppose it on the strength of that objection; not because some one else forgot to insert a provision for its adoption.

I can see no reason why a Republic cannot be maintained. True, the people must be wise and discreet in order to organize one; then they must always continue so. Every difficulty must be settled by peaceful arbitration or convention. An appeal to arms must, under no circumstances, be resorted to. No provocation should be sufficient to induce a democratic people to arm against themselves. The moment they appeal to the sword ends the Republic. The sword is the symbol of tyrants; while reason is the fountain of democracy. If you unthrone reason and let passion reign, mob-violence and terrorism prevail. These are the scourge of society, and the bane of human happiness; effects the reverse of all governments are felt.

But Democracies, and, in fact, all governments, have never been permanent. Some latent defect exists. In the bosom of the commonwealth a viper is nourished which continually gnaws at the vitals of the institution. It remains for future legislators to discover and eradicate the evil. I think it is selfishness, ambition, pride and envy. When these are removed, wars will cease, and governments will be permanent. Whether people can be wise and selfish and envious, is not for me, in this place, to determine. This, however, I will say, that a selfish people are not capable of self-government; for where all are ambitious of ruling, none can, according to the strict letter of democracy. A man must rule for the people, not for himself. He must deem his interest as secondary; and this is not the policy of selfish men. These wish to get a large slice for themselves, and, where all are grabbing for self, there is no room for the people.

The eyes of the world have been upon the American Republic from her inauguration to the present time. Some prognosticated it a failure, and thought the people incompetent to rule themselves. But time has demonstrated it to be a fact, that, in the early ages of a commonwealth, people are more virtuous and disinterested, and, therefore, more capable of governing themselves than succeeding generations. The cause of this decline in morals is owing to the prosperous condition of our finances. Could the people always remain poor, they would remain virtuous. But wealth, in general, is incompatible with strict integrity; and, as a people advances in prosperity, they decline in moral worth. If a people could be as wise in prosperity as they are brave in adversity, there would be no difficulty in maintaining democratic institutions; but to bear up with forti-

tude in adversity, and to be moderate in prosperity, are virtues which but few possess; and to ask a whole nation to endue itself with such philosophy is rather too much; at least, without more teaching and preparation. It may not be impossible, but still it is impracticable as the public mind is now constituted. Whether we would be happier under a different organization, — one more democratic, — is very obvious. But we are not to tell what government is the best, but what is the policy of our own.

Our foreign policy should be mild and conciliatory; ever ready to redress grievances, and the last to provoke aggression. We should stand on our own vantage-ground, secure within ourselves, giving an asylum to the oppressed of every clime, extending the benefits of hospitality to all who may by chance or pleasure throw themselves upon our generosity, giving aid and comfort to the down-trodden, liberating the civilly bound and the politically oppressed, and by heeding every solicitation tending to the establishment of institutions similar to our own. But we should not sow the seeds of dissension among a peaceful people; if they, like ourselves, wish to become free, we should do to them as we were pleased to have France do to us.

If the Canadian provinces revolt, and struggle manfully for a time, we should, if they seek our assistance, give it; and if they wish to enter the Union, we should allow it upon such terms as the contracting parties may engage; but because we assisted them in the acquisition of liberty and independence, even if it be known that it was mainly through our instrumentality that they acquired it, we should not for this reason force them to the acceptance of our institutions. This would not only be unjust, but unwise. We would be doing violence to our own principles in thus coercing a reluctant State; and it would be no more unjust in trying to coerce the Canadians, than it is in coercing a member of the Federal Union. The cases are analogous in principle, if not in fact. If a State has the right to accept, she has the right to reject; and if she has the right to reject at one time, she has the right to reject at any other. Time does not destroy principle; it is the same now that it ever was, and always will be as it is. Generations may come and go; seasons may roll on indefinitely, but principle remains unchanged forever.

If any State across the Atlantic desires liberty and independence, we should give them our sympathy if not aid; although we should not endeavor to corrupt the allegiance of faithful subjects. As long as they are happy, and willing to live in bondage and subjection, we should consent; but as soon as they find the yoke oppressive, and they long for a more genial air, we should rush to them with the alacrity of brothers ready and willing to bleed and die in their defence. Though there may be many moral objections against fighting, yet there are as many against slavery; and, of the two, I think slavery is the worst. It is better for a man to die, if he cannot live an honor to the race; and what is more dishonorable than to see a man crouch beneath a tyrant's rod? I had rather see him buried. I had rather see a generation annihilated, than to see it tremble in servile vassalage to the nod of a despot. As long as tyrants and oligarchies rule, there will be war. These are the cause of war; when they die, war will be no more. When men cease to oppress their fellow-beings, then both the cause and the effect will be removed. So it is useless to talk of doing away with war till the cause of it be removed. War is the lesser evil.

We can therefore hope for no alleviation of this dreadful scourge, till its cause is done away. These two principles are at war in the European and Asiatic worlds, aristocracy and democracy; and they are at war among themselves. One wishes to rear up an aristocracy on African servitude; the other, on the servitude of the white man. One would give no compensation, and the other a paltry amount, barely sufficient to keep the laborer alive. Such an aristocracy is experienced, in all its horrors, on the British Islands. Democracy is but faintly represented on the American shores; but, in Europe, there is a strong democratic element, and which is to have the mastery time only can solve. Absolute subjection or absolute freedom is the destiny of the world. Cossack tyranny or constitutional liberty. Man must obey the voice of a despot or legislate for himself. What an alternative awaits us; nay, the *world*. What a drama is enacting! We tremble for man! We would glory in his emancipation. Let us live and hope that all will be for the best. How anxiously shall we look for the consummation of the issue. Life is sweeter by wishing to see the result.

In regard to the issue now being decided by an appeal to arms, something more, perhaps, might be said with propriety. Whether it could have been settled peaceably, in the present crisis, is only conjectural. In the early ages of our commonwealth no such agitation would have disturbed the public mind. But now the people love excitement; all participate in it with glee and ardor; it is nourishment for the mind, and recreation for the body. What people desire, that, perhaps,

they ought to have. If they had been inclined to conciliate and compromise with the South, there would have been no difficulty. Many in the South and North hoped that some amicable arrangement would be adopted for the peaceable adjustment of our difficulties. Every lover of his country could not but deplore the unhappy condition of our political relations.

But how could the issue be peacefully settled, some may ask. I answer, by letting the subject alone in the States, and by leaving the people of the Territories to adopt such constitutions as they might choose. But the Northern fanatic says there is a *higher law* to be obeyed. What have higher laws to do with finite ones? Do not talk of higher laws, when yourselves are guilty of enacting lower ones. It does not become fanatics and ambitious demagogues to talk of morals, or the decrees of Omnipotence. Perfect yourselves, before you endeavor to perfect others. While such a spirit exists, it is useless to talk of compromise. People, wild with frenzy cannot reason; they must be taught by experience the error of which they have been guilty.

A line straight through to the Pacific could have been drawn, north of which could have been free, and south of it, slave. But whether the people would have lived more happily with freedom and slavery united, is not for us in this treatise to determine. It is impossible for two hostile elements to exist in the same place, at the same time, in peace, and the South, acting upon this axiom, would have adopted such measures as would gradually have rid the country of the baneful evil. If I recollect right, measures were being taken for this purpose when the anti-slavery pestilence broke out. Man is very much like a hog; he must not be urged. If they had been let alone, more would have been accomplished towards the emancipation of the slaves than will be now. Now they will only change their masters, with perhaps a paltry compensation, but they will be just as much slaves as they ever were; perhaps, more the objects of speculation and gain.

We are not discussing the moral of the institution, but simply the policy of our government. Slavery, in every form, is wrong; but I contend that the country is exchanging a lesser for a greater evil. Instead of four millions of slaves, we will have thirty; and they will be increased in the ratio of our population. When any people have gone to such a length, war is inevitable. But this is not an excuse; we should have remained at peace among ourselves. This was our policy. The doom which awaits us remains to be experienced. Few are so wise as to be lieve, even should it be told, before the actual consummation of the tragedy.

It would have been better policy to let the states go than by nullifying the fundamental principle of the constitution by coercing them into obedience. To have separated would have been the lesser evil. Then we might enact such laws as we saw fit, and they might do the same. It would soon have been evident to all that it would be more difficult to maintain amicable relations between independent states, than when united. Our foreign intercourse would be doubly expensive. All the inconvenience arising from such a state of things would be manifest to all; and all would hasten with alacrity to join their counsels in friendly blending; and they would surround themselves with new securities, thereby strengthening democratic principles, instead of weakening them. The Union would derive more glory from such a return to the bosom of the federal compact, than it is possible to acquire in any other way: it would be founded in wisdom, justice and truth; all would glory in the event.

Now it will be different. One part must be subdued, and brought by the force of might to acquiesce in the will of the stronger. This one will not be satisfied. The memory of defeat will always rankle in their bosoms; and this never will be eradicated as long, at least, as such a state of things lasts. Might

cannot always prevail; and when they find the rigor of constraint lessened, they will rise and vindicate their supremacy. They will yet be free, and so will every man.

The whole North American Continent is too large to be controlled by one government. There should then be one government at the north, and one at the south. Let those states that wish to go with the south, go; and those that wish to stay with the north, stay, and let the south have Washington; and let the north rear one, rivalling Constantinople, somewhere near the great lakes. There is no use of fighting in order to hold together reluctant states; it cannot be done. The great Roman Empire could not be held together by force. The fragments will fall off one by one in spite of arms. Then why destroy your sons, and expend your treasure in a useless contest? Be more wise and considerate. You may triumph for the moment, so did Cæsar. You may display your greatness, so did Cæsar; but where now is Cæsar, and Rome's greatness? Where is her empire? Where is the respect she once inspired? Do you wish to follow her foot steps? Go on. Do you wish to rise like her that you may fall like her? Do you wish to make your glory so manifest that your shame ca nnot cover it? If so, pursue the path you are on; it will lead to an oblivious grave.

March 20, 1865.

APPENDIX.

Since the foregoing was written, great and important changes have come to pass. A few short months have solved a world of mystery. The rebel army has been defeated, and is now disbanded. The chief of the insurgent states is in confinement, awaiting his doom at the bar of his country. The chief of constitutional authority has already met his at the hands of a foul murderer. President Johnson has been inaugurated as chief of the American Republic. Measures are being taken for the re-adjustment of our national difficulties. Disfranchisement of the insurrectionists is one of the schemes of abolitionists; and negro suffrage another; miscegenation another fanatical illustration of a disordered intellect.

These subjects seem to demand more than a passing notice in this place; and, on account of the importance of the issues involved, I have resolved to append a few paragraphs to this pamphlet before sending it to press.

PREFACE.

It will be observed that it is written in defence of secession, or the rights of states, or individual sovereignty; that the right of secession has already been negatived by the bayonet; and that many propositions which I have advanced have also proved untrue thus far. In regard of this I will say first in this place, what I said before, that might is sometimes right, but not always. But might cannot decide the abstract right or wrong of an idea; and if it does, it only presumes, and is only apparent. Right is right, whatever the voice of man may pronounce; or the hand of man execute. In regard to that proposition which declares the necessity of keeping a standing army in order to hold the conquered provinces in subjection, just imbitter the pangs of defeat by adding the reproach of weakness, lack of bravery, ingratitude to country, home, and family, and you will see how quick the eye will flash with indignation, and the lips curl with rage. The fanatic says let them; they cannot help themselves; they must submit; live under the yoke, and groan. Say not so, my deluded friend. "He that conquers the body subdues but half his foe." Americans are not Hungarians, nor Poles who are now groaning in just such slavery to which abolition demagoguism would reduce a moiety of the American people. If a miraculous interposition of Providence had not at this time manifested itself, I know not what would have befallen us. This, you recollect, I said would save us.

PRESIDENT'S ASSASSINATION.

But was the assassination of the President a miraculous intervention? I think it was; had it not been, it would not have been committed. What end God wished to bring about by bringing such a calamity upon us, is not for me to determine. Nor should we call that a calamity which God chooses to inflict. It might have been a blessing, but how? Would he not have settled our differences as successfully as President Johnson? Was he not as wise and prudent a statesman as Johnson? Would he not have received the vanquished enemy with the same clemency and forgiving mercy? His course, judging by past examples, would have been to advance the interests of the country, and not to pursue with revengeful malice the enemies of his party. Whether we are blessed by the change of masters, or by his tragical and lamentable death, is a question which can now never be solved. There is only one issue before us — his death. What he would have done, had he lived, can now be only conjectured. That he was the best friend the enemy had is conceded by all. Then it must be that we are blessed more by his death than we would have been by his life; for God surely would choose the most efficacious means to effect a given end; and God's ends are good, consequently it was good that Lincoln was thus cruelly dispatched. It is hard to reconcile ourselves to such a conclusion. To think it better that such a good man, such a disinterested statesman should be taken from us, and we left alone to find our way through such a troubled world amidst toils and difficulties innumerable, is impossible to reconcile with our stricken hearts. We are overwhelmed with grief and sorrow; yet we find consolation in the thought that God's eye saw it, and His over-ruling providence directed it.

IMMODERATE EXULTATION.

The armies of the Union were fast encircling the heroic band in their defence of the shattered remnants of the insurgents' strength. One after another fell into the meshes of military strategy; and soon, it was rumored, the hydra must succumb to the repeated assaults of our army. The bells began to ring, and the cannon to echo forth the joyous sound of victory. The people were delirious with joy. They met but to congratulate each other on the happy termination of internecine strife. Shouts of joy and prayers of thanksgiving ascended together to the throne of a righteous Judge. Hymns of praise and the glad hosanna resounded through the land. God could but look down upon such a scene with indignant pity. Man was triumphing over his fellow-man, and rejoicing in his fall. He saw a great people, intelligent, brave and magnanimous, rejoicing over their own discomfiture and ruin.

EXECRATION OF THE MURDERER.

What could He do to bring them to a sense of their error, and set them in the path of duty? He had not to consider long. The chief is mortal, and at His disposal. Him, as the idol of the immoderately joyous people, He resolves to strike down. There was not another individual in the United States, no, nor in the world, whom he could remove and afflict the people so deeply. He was the corner stone of the nation; to remove him would wound them in the most sensitive, yet not fatal part. In a moment, in a twinkling, when all is buoyant with the happiest anticipations, when joy and mirth reign supreme, when not a thought of danger disturbed sleeping millions, the fatal blow was struck. First, the rumor flashed through the land, but none believed. Humanity was shocked. Men stood appalled in horror. Next came the confirmation with particulars. Some believed; many discredited; and many hoped the next telegraph would give a different report — one at least mitigating the dreadful calamity. It could not be fatal. He still lives. No, no, I will not credit it; it cannot be. The President dead — struck down in the bosom of his family by a fell and murderous attack of a man! O, ungrateful wretch! Foul blot on America's noble, and heretofore, untarnished escutcheon. He

was the chief of the people; the father, as it were, of a great family. He reposed implicit confidence in each member thereof. He thought none so brutal and traitorous as to plunge a dagger into his heart. He who had wronged no one as the representative of the people, in the discharge of delegated authority, is struck down, and in a few hours is dead. Without the least thought, or apprehension of danger, he is launched into the presence of an avenging God. Not a moment is given him to consider his end. He was shot in the head while viewing a theatrical scene.

EULOGY ON PRESIDENT LINCOLN.

Thus perished the chief of a great Republic. It is the first instance of the kind that has occurred in our history. Some have died while in the discharge of executive duties on beds of sickness; but none of them were thus tragically dispatched. The people were never before plunged so deep in corruption as to take the life of the chief magistrate. It has learned us a lesson which I hope we will profit by, and never again to engage in such a strife, sure to bring with it such calamities. It demonstrates that war breeds war, as like begets like, and that those who favor strife and bloodshed will, sooner or later, be made to feel its effects. The strife is not ended yet; though a good deal depends on the measures adopted by the executive. If these be stringent, severe, and exemplary, you may rest assured that the reign of terror is not yet begun; but it would be sure to succeed such steps as fanatics would take; for the same weapons of sanguinary vengeance can be wielded by the defeated party, almost as successfully as they can by constituted authorities; and this, I think, would be right. It is right that the same means which are adopted to re-organize civil authority, should recoil upon itself. This is to be expected. It behooves the administration to be lenient, merciful, and just; and, if we should judge from past measures, this is the course which it will pursue. If the enemy be so ungrateful as not to reciprocate such treatment, then theirs will be the punishment, not ours.

There is another fact to be noticed as a result from this mournful tragedy. It is this: The nation was in a paroxysm of joy. The banners floated proudly out in the breeze, decorated with emblems of national triumph. Bands of music pealed forth national airs. All was redolent with joy. In a moment an ominous silence pervades. The music ceases. The bells are hushed; and the cannon no longer sends forth its cheering accents far and wide. The flag, so shortly before

~en waving in all the splendor of national glory, droops and falls half way to the ground, as if shorn of its strength. Faintly it flutters in the chilly air, its majesty hidden by the bordering crape.

But what? what does all this mean? *The President is dead!!* An audible murmur is the only response. The nation weeps such tears as never before were shed upon American soil. Faction is hushed up and from all parts of the land the same feelings are manifested. All drop a tear of regret upon the grave of the departed martyr, and execrate the perpetrators of the fiendish act. Friend and foe; freeman and serf alike bewail his end. Dastardly is that wretch, who, from partisan motives, fails to lament such a catastrophe. Every one should lament it for two reasons, first: he should regret that the nation has become so corrupt as in it to find one mean and depraved enough to commit such a fiendish crime; and secondly: he should lament that such an object should be chosen on whom to wreak such ferocious vengeance — one the least guilty of all the nation. He was only doing the will of the people; he was their servant, and yet their head. He was in the discharge of legitimate authority. It was not his own doing, but the doings of the people. It was not his own will, but theirs. He was not the cause of the calamities which were being visited upon the people; they were the cause of their own suffering; they were inflicting on themselves the chastening rod. If he would not consent to serve in that capacity, others could be found sufficiently brave to take upon themselves the discharge of those duties which appertain to the executive. Should a man be thus foully murdered for committing no crime, save that of being the chosen chief of a great people? Should he suffer for the errors of which the people are guilty? Should he be punished for their transgressions? Could he take upon himself the sins of the people and expiate them by yielding up his life?

If such were the end and duty of presidents, few would be the aspirants for a martyr's grave. The office would not be one which ambition would seek, but to which culprits would be condemned. No haste nor solicitation would be manifested. There would be no anxiety to know the result of the elections. There would be no lingering at the polls at night to learn the exact truth. If the one must go who has the most friends, he could but regret being blessed by such a curse. We are afraid that conventions would be very thinly attended, in the fear that their presence might remind some enemy of some slight or affront, who would take the present opportunity to be avenged. It would be a place where, of all others in the world, few would congregate.

Such, we think, is the reason why God chose to chasten this people. They were immoderately joyous previous to, and at the time of his death; but since this mournful event not an exultant sound has been heard. The enemies' empire has gone on crumbling without eliciting the least applause; now, not a single defiant stronghold exists to menace the liberty, or endanger the peace of the citizens. No triumphs for these successes; no gladsome shouts; no hymns of praise; no prayers of thanksgiving. No smile of approbation lights up the countenance; but in sadness every one receives the melancholy news; no longer manifesting any interest in the termination of national difficulties. So deep are the people sunk in sorrow that they find no contentment in resignation, and refuse absolutely to be comforted, or raised from their despondency. They can take no pleasure in triumphs unless enjoyed by him who so gloriously conducted the campaign. With him they could enjoy all; without him nothing.

I think if the people had been more moderate in success, or had rejoiced not at all, or philosophically regretted their brothers' overthrow, Lincoln would still have been alive. This feeling on the part of friends, would have dulled the scimitar's point, and utterly disarmed the assassin's rage. "No," some one says, "this could not be," "for it was so ordained from the beginning, that he should die such a death and in such a cause." Then if God has this foreknowledge, which he has if he is Omniscient, He must also have known that the people would make fools of themselves in going beyond all bounds in exulting over the fall of their brothers, thereby giving a cause and an excuse to an event, which could not by any possibility happen from chance. It was God's doing, and he foreordained the whole. He designed it for our good, as all things which come from God are good. His dispensations are just. If we transgress a physical law, we must suffer in sickness. Our punishment is inevitable. It is as sure to follow as night is day. We cannot evade it. Were it not for these transgressions there would be no sickness, as man would live to a green old age, to drop at last into a welcomed grave.

MORAL TRANSGRESSIONS PUNISHED.

Just so in the moral world; though the punishment is not so evident, yet it must follow. Man is always more affected by sensible things than by things intangible. He is almost driven to the belief that the sensible is all in all; and that everything else exists but in the imagination of men. He does not know that he can be morally afflicted; neither does he know that an affliction is a necessary result for the breach of a moral law. He may lose his wife, or be maimed; or his children suffer some mishap, as an eye may be put out, an ear lost, or both; a leg or an arm may be broken, or his understanding may fail, still he will not attribute these disasters to any breach of moral duty. But if he eat cucumbers, or some other of the vegetable kingdom, and they cause him distress, he immediately refers the cause of it to the fact that he ate cucumbers. Here are cause and effect that are plain and unmistakable. It requires no argument whatever to prove it; he knows it to be a fact.

This I presume is the cause why many are thrown from affluence to poverty and want; and why many are unexpectedly rewarded with a large fortune, or some other great and important success in life. Abundant examples may be elicited in proof of both of these points. We see them every day. They are so common that they cease to attract attention. We see one rise up, apparently without any effort, to occupy important positions in society and the world; while another sinks down to the level from which an upstart just rose. Another may struggle on through life honestly and bravely, and barely live from hand to mouth, but meet with no startling success. Another may build himself up by illicit traffic and dishonest gains, and no great mishap befall him. He may lie, and cheat, and swear, and take usurious interest, to an enormous extent, passing through life successfully, and finally die and sink into a sinner's grave, a curse to himself, a curse to the world, and a curse to his God. But this does not disprove the hypothesis; he may yet have to answer for his crimes. His children may rise up and walk in the paths of rectitude, honor, and truth; but more likely they will follow the paths, or some of them, which their fathers trod. A man might as well be guilty of every vice as to be guilty of one. But " the iniquities of the father shall be visited unto the third and fourth generation." If a sinner pass through life successfully, look and see whether his children or grand-children do or not.

IS PRESIDENT DAVIS GUILTY ?

As we have exonerated President Lincoln from all fault, so we must President Davis. As the former is but the instrument in the hand of God for the purpose of working out the destiny of the people, so Davis is but the rod with which God chastens the people. Had he not been the instrument

some one else would. His non-acceptance of the trust would not have prevented the catastrophe. The people are, in such cases, answerable for the safety and well-being of him whom they clothe with their authority, provided only that he does not transcend it. True, if I instigate a people to revolt, I am amenable to a law; but in this case I would not be committing a crime which would be unpardonable. I might be instigated by an impracticable patriotism. I might be a zealous expounder of some abstract truth, and which, by success might drive me beyond all bounds, and precipitate me in the vortex of popular enthusiasm. In this case, I should seem to be carried along, rather than leading them from their duty and allegiance into rebellion. Still I may be guilty of exciting them in the first instance, but, I would not be, for consequences which I did not intend nor foresee, but were rather the result of circumstances. But when a people rise up in all their majesty, and fanatical zeal, and select one resident in their midst to lead them for better or worse, I believe it his duty to accept, and exert all his energies for the well-being of that people. Let the insurrection be great or small, the case is exactly the same. Man owes allegiance first to his family, then to his immediate surroundings; then, if he wishes, and it is desired of him, to a distant Government. If a man be attacked in his household by a party of banditti, he does not wait to consult the Government, nor the civil authorities, to ascertain if he have a right to drive them with violence from his premises, or lay them in the dust. By the time an answer is returned the necessity for action is passed, and there is nothing to do about the matter, unless to arraign and convict the murderers. The necessities of the case preclude the possibility of consulting any other law, or rule of action, than that which immediately presents itself. A man owes duty and allegiance to nothing which cannot protect him in the enjoyment of life and liberty. What can Government, or law, do for me in the midst of a mob ? Then I am thrown upon my own resources, and any course which I may pursue to effect my deliverance, the same is right and just. Law does not pretend to protect its citizens in cases of a mob or riot; nor is there any moral difference when a people rise and declare their allegiance withdrawn from an existing authority, and at the same time clothe one of their number with that allegiance.

It is his duty to accept such trust; for he may, if he be wise and prudent, be able to lead them through much happier than if Jacobin fury rule. What would France have done in '93 had not Napoleon been there ? He was the restorer of law and order, and was the blessing of the people; whereas, had he not taken upon himself the discharge of executive duties, untold miseries would have been the lot of the French. Such is the duty of man in any and every such case. Suppose he refuse, and try to resist the impetuosity of the people, his life and possessions may be endangered, or he driven into ignominious exile. A man might as well try to stay with his hands the waves of the sea. It is better, too, to have a recognized head in all such undertakings; it is better for the people at home, and for the people abroad. He is the administrator of law at home, and the negotiator with friends and enemies abroad. Suppose there had been no head of the Southern Confederacy; suppose the executive duties had been performed by a convention, similar to that which sat upon the destinies of the French people, what would have been the result? Would the contest have been less ferocious and sanguinary? Would the horrors of war have been mitigated? Would it have been more easily terminated? It may have been terminated more speedily, but, while it lasted, it would have been terribly bloody. It would have exceeded in savage ferociousness the French reign of terror, and the most terrible deaths would have been inflicted upon prisoners. None would be permitted to escape their fury. Untold woes would have been the lot of the Southern people. If we consider the subject thoroughly it will be found better for the North, and better for the South, better for all concerned.

WHAT SHALL BE DONE WITH HIM?

Now the question arises, shall we hang the man for making it better? For being an instrument in the hands of God for the purpose of working out the salvation of the people. What has he done, or what crime has he committed? Alas! none can be shown. Some cry treason! treason! but who has committed treason? The constitution says that "treason shall consist in actually levying war against the United States, or in aiding or in abetting their enemies." Now who has levied war? No one individually. The people rose up in mass and commanded him whom they delegated to lead them against their enemies. But first they must be organized, equipped, and drilled; and every means that will conduce to this end is also conceded. Now for him simply to have exercised these powers, is no more treason then to organize a squad of men who are desirous of working so that they may work to the best advantage. The people may be guilty of treason and rebellion, but no single man is; for no one man could raise up such

5

a gigantic insurrection. And if you think of punishing the people for doing that which every true lover of his country claims to have the right to do, you will have a hard task; for no American will support an iniquitous usurpation, and one directly opposed to the genius of American institutions.

Suppose you try him, and adjudge him guilty, and hang him, what then? Would it nullify his acts or his pretensions? Would it deter others from assuming in like cases the same responsibilities? Certainly not. Such punishments have been inflicted for thousands of years, still the crime goes on. Then why not begin to adopt other measures, and see if a better result is not the reward. As for nullifying State rights, or individual sovereignty, it is out of the question. It is inherent. You might as well try to unmake yourself, and condemn the whole human race to the sphere of the phenomenal. You may as well proclaim his mortality, the non-existence of a God, and an hundred other like absurdities, which only prove the ignorance and arrogance of a presuming fanatic. Such things do not destroy eternal principles. They will live forever in spite of man. And if he dies for this, he is a martyr to the truth. His grave will be decked with flowers, and his fate bewailed by the tears of millions. His courage in the hour of peril, his moderation in the hour of victory; and his fortitude in the hour of distress, will be recounted as an illustration of the most remarkable virtues manifested during this trying period.

TO DIE FOR TRUTH, GLORIOUS.

How resigned he should be in view of such a glorious end! To die for the truth has been the glory of but a few. But few are esteemed worthy of a martyr's crown. How gladly would I lay down all I possess in the defence of such a principle. Gladly would I change places with the prisoner, if I could but be worthy of such an end. If he is guilty then I am, and every one who maintains his innocence. I would commit myself as he has without the least hesitation. I would do again what he has already done, and for which he now stands accused. On this I have planted my resolution, to live in the maintenance of democratic institutions, and if need be, die in their defence. A democrat I was born, and a democrat I will die, let who will reign, reign.

Our fathers fought and died in the defence of this principle, and shall we, ungrateful sons of honored sires, throw away or ignore it? Never! Let Americans always be true to themselves, if they wish to be respected and loved. Let us never sully the fair fame which crowns the American name. Let us never ignore those cherished principles which are the pride of our life; the bulwark of our strength; and the basis on which our constitution is founded. They are our all. Take them away and we are shorn of our majesty and strength, and left desolate upon nothing. Let the world go on as it will, but let Americans live absolute upon their own vantage ground, strong in the consciousness of inherent worth; ever walking in the paths of truth, justice, honor, and love.

In the decision on his case rests the abstract right of individual sovereignty; and in deciding it the judiciary will have need of all circumspection lest they commit treason against themselves, and nullify the rights of Americans, or set at naught the liberty won by our ancestors upon the bloody field. Soon this great question will be solved theoretically, if not judicially. O Americans! let not the stain of this man's blood be upon us. Let not this blighting curse go down to posterity, that we could prove ungrateful to ourselves, our country, and to our God. Let us not stamp the valor of our fathers with infamy. But let us crown their patriotism with the never fading wreath of clemency and mercy. Let us be merciful to the vanquished, and forgive them, if they be guilty, as we hope sometime to be forgiven.

ANOTHER CONSIDERATION.

There is another feature to be examined in connection with the change of chiefs which was thus tragically brought about. It is thought by some that Lincoln would be too lenient and merciful to the conquered rebels, and therefore to punish them the more, God thought best to remove him, and substitute another in his stead. This one, they thought, had been sufficiently aggrieved by the suppliant and misguided enemy, to pursue them with remorseless vengeance. They, the left wing of the now so called republican or abolition party, thought to make them feel bitterly the pangs of defeat; and they consoled themselves for the death of their favorite, by thinking that he had finished his work, and that it was necessary for another, who, from recent ill treatment, and partisan antipathies, was rendered particularly odious to them, to take the helm of state and guide her through her voyage. They thought that his feelings were sufficiently imbittered from these causes to drive him into acts which a less irritated mind would detest; and which he himself would not do under other circumstances. They wished to have them disfranchised; their lands and goods confiscated,

and they left to wander about in want of the necessaries of life; and in subjection to their slaves! This is the scheme which was now concocted, and which was their consolation in the hour of bereavement.

They had already found that Lincoln was too good to betray his country into the hands of unprincipled fanatics; and they thought every one would have scruples about carrying out such unpatriotic and partisan measures; whose judgment would not be tortured by the recollection of personal indignities, and undisguised taunts; and for this reason they searched the country through and through to find one who, in case of such an accident as the death of the president, might be sufficiently subservient to their wishes as to wield the rod of oppression over the conquered states. Him they found in Andrew Johnson, of Tennessee; a man, who of all others in the United States, is best adapted for the work to which he is assigned. He would, like Nero, make the enemy feel themselves die. He would take pleasure in seeing them writhe beneath the heel of oppression. He would be deaf to all entreaties. His heart would be hardened by the remembrance of past insults, and his soul would be inaccessible to pity. No tears could move the iron resolution of his will. No supplications, however prostrate and humble, could bend him from his purpose. He had been wronged and he must be avenged. The groans, and tears, and sighs of millions, must be spent in vain to gratify personal resentments. He is the James II. of the American revolution. A Jeffries would soon be found to execute his merciless mandates. This doctrine I heard preached over the cold remains of the martyred president. It shows to what a pitch of arrogance success will carry the fanatic. A calm and dispassionate mind cannot but deplore the sad condition into which we have fallen, by allowing partisan prejudices to carry us so far beyond the limits of reason.

The extreme North is as far from the right as the extreme South. The latter had negro slaves; and the former would reverse the position of the parties, — making whites the slaves with negroes for their masters. Which would be the worst of the two, remains happily to be seen; but that neither will result is my anxious hope and wish. A wise and judicious man will condemn both, and mark out for his course a path equi-distant from the two extremes. Each is equally far from the mean, and therefore equally wrong; and the only true patriotic position for one to take, is that which president Johnson is now following, however unpleasant it may be to the radical portion of the community.

Such was the bitterness of party spirit which manifested itself, in a greater or less degree, from all quarters of the Union on the assumption of the President of the executive duties of the Nation. But imagine their surprise when the first kneeling supplicant was raised by a brotherly hand, and assured that he would be protected in all the privileges and immunities of an American citizen. Imagine a grateful heart overflowing with love for that great man whom that heart had once so indiscreetly wronged. How the tears flowed down that emaciated face, made so by fear and anxiety for his fate, and the fate of his friends, and the fate of his beloved country, — for the love of which he had been led so far away into the paths of rebellion and war; instigated by a misguided patriotism, harrowed up to the highest pitch of frenzy and despair, and goaded on by zeal for party aggrandizement, and the extinction of antagonistical factions. Beams of joy light up his haggard countenance. Smiles play in fitful flashes where but a short time ago sat despair in all its horror. Sunshine and hope now radiate from his being, and he is again a man, elevated from a worse end than a grave — a living, a slow, consuming remorse.

EULOGY ON PRESIDENT JOHNSON.

God be praised for this deliverance — for this great prodigy of a man. He is our country's glory, and our country's salvation. Wisdom, and justice, and clemency reign in his heart. When we least expected, and least merited such a deliverer, God graciously presents him to us for our salvation. Let us try and appreciate the wonderful combination of the most heroic and commendable qualities with which God has endowed him. Let us return our most grateful thanks to Him for this great blessing. He has blessed us with peace, and has blessed us with a great and a noble President. Under his fostering care we shall have Union, and concord, and a glorious prosperity. Our hill sides shall again bloom; our valleys shall again return us a plenteous harvest. The sun shall again shine in splendor upon our happy homes; and peace shall reign in all our borders. My own, my beautiful America! Thou land of the free, or grave of the brave; long have you been torn by intestine broils through the mad folly of your misguided sons. Now let peace, union, and happiness reign.

INVOLUNTARY SERVITUDE DEAD.

The conquered enemies come to him with the firm assurance that justice will be awarded them. All that they desire and expect

is freely given. The cause of the strife is conceded as lost. They neither advocate now, nor wish to hear it mentioned. They took up arms like patriots and men, in the defence of a cherished and immemorial institution. This institution they believed to be right; and they thought that if it was right it could be maintained and established on a firmer foundation by might. They resolved upon the struggle. They fought bravely, as became the sons of revolutionary sires, in the defence of what they thought was right. The issue was tried; and the issue is lost, and they manfully give it. They fought like patriots, and now like patriots they sue for peace. A patriot extends them this hallowed boon with a fraternal hand, and assures them that they are Americans still entitled to all the prerogatives of citizenship. These they accept with a grateful heart, remembering that the fate of the conquered is in the hands of the conqueror, and that their all is at his disposal. How modestly he wields these great powers, condescending to the condition of the meanest vassal to accept from their hands a suffrage. He graciously gives to them the power to thwart all his measures, and defeat himself, when it lays in his power to retain it. How magnanimous! How unselfish! Even while the mad hue-and-cry of faction is ringing in his ears — disfranchise them! Grind them in the dust! and make them feel their humiliation by putting into the hands of an uneducated, arrogant, and stupid race the rod of oppression. How merciful he is to permit these wild fanatics to continue their demoralizing and partisan schemes.

But some of them say he cannot help himself, — he who so patriotically disarms himself in the presence of hostile foes, and trusts to the honor and magnanimity of the people for that support and encouragement which he merits. Do you say he cannot help himself? O, thou dastard! How unworthy American Liberty! To see a man, strong in the knowledge of conscious worth, throw himself wholly upon the people, and rest his cause upon their decision, without the aid of a supporting arm, relying implicitly upon their love of democratic principles, made sweet and more impressive by the recollection of revolutionary glory, is truly the noblest act in the history of American independence. To see a man, armed by the strength of a million bayonets, throw them all aside and depend upon the justice of his cause, received from the hands of a discerning people, is placing a confidence in the love of the popular heart never before equalled; and it shows, on his part, a deep love of justice, truth, and liberty never before surpassed.

WASHINGTON AND JOHNSON COMPARED.

You say Washington voluntarily resigned absolute authority. True; but over what did he have absolute authority? Thirteen colonies reduced to starvation and beggary. Their promise to pay was considered worthless. The army was miserably fed, clothed, and never paid; but they were patriots, who never complained of the injustice done them by their country. To have laid down such authority, I should have esteemed a great privilege. The happiness of domestic peace, under the peaceful shades of Mount Vernon, could not be found in the contending factions; nor in the turmoil of political responsibilities. But to see a man lay down authority that is worth keeping argues the highest patriotism, and the greatest confidence in the people and nation whose navies whiten every sea; and whose cannons speak terror and defiance in the ears of tyrants. Then we were loved and respected by none; now we are feared and reverenced by all. Then we were rising into existence; now we have grown to our strength. Then we were infants; now we are men; though not yet arrived to that majesty and stateliness of gray-headed old age. We have seen the navy almost disbanded. It was the pride and glory of the American name. It was a shield in war, and a lion in peace. She protected us from insults, and avenged our injuries. But now, relying upon our internal strength, and the consciousness that we will do right in all cases and award justice to every party, he trusts himself upon the judgment of the people in the firm belief that they will not do violence to themselves. His cause is theirs. Without them, his titles would be but a shadow, and his reward would be nothing. They are the sovereign, and he is their servant. This position he chose rather than be their master and his country's ruin. Never in the annals of the human race was such devotedness so amply illustrated. He has entirely forgotten himself in his love for his country, — the people are his country, — and their wishes are the rule of his acts. They are his judges and arbitrators. They hold in their hands the keys of their salvation, and his fate. In their decision he trusts; in their wisdom he hopes and confides.

Washington had no partisan enmities to reconcile. True he had a government to form and laws to promulgate. These could be accomplished by calm reasoning and patient toil. No enemies at home, and no false friends to counteract his work. He had not to fear the dagger of the assassin. He felt himself safe while enduring every hardship. He could lie down and repose sweetly at night, after a hard day's toil. But now the case is different. The president has as hard, if not harder, work to perform, and this must be done surrounded by the most insuperable difficulties. He has enmities to reconcile; claims to adjust; friends to gratify; enemies to appease; four millions of negroes to protect from the avariciousness of their friends, and make them useful to the state; some he feels it his duty to conciliate; others to soothe; and others to force into obedience; and all this must be done for the good of the state, and to the honor of himself. Surely, it is a greater work than ever a man contemplated.

DISFRANCHISEMENT.

We can see how uncharitable the friends of the negro are in the fact that they can consciously urge upon the president the necessity of taking from their late brethren in arms the right of the elective franchise, — a right which was obtained by the blood of our fathers, and bequeathed in common to us, their children. Would we take from one another a right which we all equally enjoy? O how mean! But why are they so solicitous on this subject? Because it takes from their fellow brethren their most potent shield. They would have him completely disarmed and at their mercy. They fear that if they have a right to elect delegates to their congress, they may thwart their schemes, and ultimately acquire political preponderance. Such a contingency they cannot think of without the most serious apprehensions. Perhaps, in their despair, they might accept the arbitration of the sword, and maintain those very rights which they now ignore. The future is shrouded in mystery, neither can we draw aside the vail, nor peep through; but a few years will disclose much, which it is worth living to learn.

What other object they can have in view, than the maintainance of themselves, we cannot see. It surely is not designed to deter them or others from appealing to the sword; for the punishment would only aggravate the offence, and make it more likely that the oppressed would rise, after they had repaired the ravages of war, and appeal again to arms. Such an appeal could not be decided either way till after a long, and, perhaps, bloody war. The fortune of war is as fickle as all other fortunes, and it might be decided unfavorably to them. Therefore, I think it would be better not to drive them to such an extremity; still they can do, when they have the power, just as they think best. But it shows to what an extent they would carry party resentments. They know that such feelings were the cause of the war; and they seem to wish to make them the cause of another. How unwise and unpatriotic such motives are every one can see. For two reasons such a step would be impolitic. First: It would the sooner provoke another war; and secondly, that war would be doubtful. Every one who seeks the welfare of his country would not strive to plunge her into war. Therefore such feelings are instigated only by partisan revenge, or in order to maintain themselves in power.

PRECEDENT NOT FOUND.

If you look for precedent in support of such a scheme, it cannot be found; for in no instance has a nation been debarred the right of the elective franchise since the introduction of a representative government; and it has existed in some form or another for the last three thousand years. No political offence has been deemed of sufficient magnitude to be expiated by the infliction of such a punishment upon extensive territories. A portion of the rebellious Israelites was overwhelmed with destruction. This was preferable to living in abject servitude. I would rather see the whole South sink into irrevocable oblivion than see them live in crouching, trembling obedience to a lordly despot. And such a course would be as dishonorable to the supporters and perpetrators of such a scheme as to the sufferers themselves. They would look with complacency upon a prostrate man. O! how unworthy Americans and American glory. It would be more to our honor, and it would resound more to our glory to precipitate the whole South into the ocean. If a people in arms knew that such a doom awaited them, I think they would be justified in warring to the direst extremity, yea, in carrying devastation, blood, carnage, and death into the ranks, or country, of their oppressors. Let my liberty be endangered, or my disfranchisement threatened, and I think dismay would possess the souls of my persecutors, if I could inspire others with an equal zeal and noble despair. True I might be crushed, as many other patriots have been; but my fall would be glorious. Look at Poland and Hungaria! is their position an honor to Europe, and is it glorious to themselves? Nay, it is the foulest stigma upon the European system. Do you wish to see Americans, the pride and glory of the human race, reduced by Americans to the same humiliating condition? Let us live men and not tarnish the fair escutcheon of our national history. Let us keep intact our great reputation, and not do anything nor advise anything which will tend to lessen the admiration of the surrounding nations of the world. Let us keep our institutions, as they have heretofore been, the model of all representative governments. Let all nations look up to us as the authors of the most salutary laws, and the dispensers of equal justice. Let us, on all occasions, challenge the respect and esteem of every one.

THE REPUBLIC OF GREECE.

The republics of Greece were far different from ours. As soon as a province was conquered, and, unless the people were very tractable and easily subdued, a governor was immediately appointed to administer the affairs of the city. But it was not always done as a punishment; for the conquered people might previously have had no intercourse with their conquerors. If a city rebelled, the most stringent measures were adopted to hold it in obedience. The administration of the affairs of Athens was of no greater magnitude than those of New York; and if she did not extend the same liberties to her allies and friends, she enjoyed absolute liberty within the precincts of her city. True, some were ostracised for political principles; and some rogues were outlawed; but all possessed the right of the elective franchise who had arrived at the age prescribed by law, or those who were not denizens. The empire of Athens was built up and sustained by the help of her allies, each of which was sovereign and independent, though paying tribute to Athens. Each could carry on a war with a neighbor without the advice, or consent, or aid of Athens, provided only that that neighbor was not in alliance with her.

REPUBLIC OF ROME.

Rome's institutions were somewhat similar, though more despotic over her provinces and colonies. Her allies were powerful and independent kings; but when conquered they were but vassals of the Roman empire, without a voice in the councils of the state, or in the administration of justice. They were but tributary slaves. But within the walls of Rome absolute republican equality was tolerated up to the time of the emperors. We conclude hence that their institutions and ours are very dissimilar. They gave the elective franchise to whom they wished, and withheld it from whom they wished. It was not withheld from rebellious provinces oftener than it was from conquered ones. If an enemy proved valiant and struggled courageously to the last, they would add to the sting of defeat the reproach of a foreign governor. They strove to remind them continually of their subjection. Republicanism did not extend beyond the Romans themselves; nor was it taken from them till they lost it by their own indiscretion and folly. So long as they remained virtuous they were victorious and they triumphed over all enemies abroad, and kept their own selfish propensities under control. They at last conquered themselves, and they lost by their inordinate ambition that which the most powerful kings of earth had been unable to take away or destroy. So long as they remained friends to themselves, so long the world obeyed their mandates. But when the power of faction usurped dominion they fell of their own corruption.

Her fall should be a lesson to us. Let us profit by the history of her rise and fall. Let no partisan motives taint our patriotism, and be mindful of the duty which we owe ourselves. So long as we are friends to ourselves we are friends to the country. Let us do no injustice to one another; but let us strive in offices of good-will to one another how we may mitigate the necessary evils of our existence. Let us not take liberty from ourselves, then we will be sure that we are free, for no one, or no combination of kingdoms can take it from us, if we be true to ourselves.

But the course which faction and partisan warfare are now endeavoring to lead will ultimately result in our ruin. We shall have destroyed ourselves through the triumph of one faction over another, until all finally see themselves trampling upon the greatest and best institutions the genius of man ever conceived. If we are wise we will prevent this sad catastrophy by adopting such measures, and electing such men as will subserve to our general interests; and promote our national glory. If we decide to do these things all may yet be well; but should we, like Augustus, proscribe the friends of the opposition, we may rest assured that our doom is sealed, and our disgraceful oblivion, certain.

Augustus would be avenged upon the murderers of his father; and his father was the father of the Roman people. He did not interpose a word for the life of the renowned Cicero, though it was in his power to prevent his assassination.

His fourteen Philippics against Antony could not be so easily forgotten; nor could Augustus believe that he was necessary to the stability of the Roman empire, though he was the strongest prop of the state. Had Antony forgiven his powerful opponent, and all feelings of revenge been erased from the mind of Augustus and all other leading statesmen, the Roman empire might still have been

in existence. But no, the minds of men must have satisfaction for injuries received. " An eye for an eye, and a tooth for a tooth," is still the raging mania. People seem unwilling to appeal to any other resort. They do not seem to recognize in it the forerunner of their own destruction. You speak of their being injured more deeply than they injure their foe; why, they would laugh you to scorn. How can I be injured by striking that villain who so foully wronged me? It gives immediate satisfaction to the mind, yet history shows that it results disastrously to the state. When Cæsar fell the people mourned, and were sincere in their grief. To punish his murderers was to punish the enemies of the state. The enemies of Augustus were the murderers of Cæsar, and to remove these the people coöperated. Augustus gladly accepted their aid; for when all the opposition was put down nothing but servile acquiescence to his rule could be expected. Thus the people were the cause of their own enslavement. Milton says, they were "deservedly made vassal." Be careful lest we, in punishing our enemies put down the friends of the country. For fear that one friend fall a victim to our vengeance, better let two enemies escape; for one prop taken from beneath this stupendous fabric endangers its fall. Let enemies assault the outer walls to their heart's content, they cannot scale the battlements of the constitution, if we remain united, and do not, through indiscretion, sap its foundations ourselves.

OUR DUTY TO OUR COUNTRY.

Suppose you go on and proscribe the principles in this rebellion; what then? Do you think you have nullified the right of secession, and crushed forever the highest aspirations of the human heart? Or do you contend that the opposition being put down, the country will rest in peace? Fallacious hope! Do you think that the recollection of your proscription or injustice will be buried with your unsuccessful antagonists? It will live forever in the minds of orphans and widows, and revenge is just as legitimate in their hands as in yours; and if you assume the right, you must concede it to them. In this case you will bequeath a curse instead of a blessing to your children. You will make them reap in bitterness and woe the fruits of your folly. And it is better to proscribe at once the whole Southern people, than to permit them to live in servile vassalage, a disgrace to you, and a shame to them. They would be a living monument of your ingratitude to your fellow. Better, far better bury all thoughts of revenge, and return to the support of our common country. Let us unite ourselves together in social, endearing friendship.

If we cannot be perfect, we can make another advance toward that end ; but no one will ever arrive there, so long as the unhallowed lusts of the sensible world are the end of his endeavors. Are we going to stand still in the advance already made, and not make another exertion towards the perfection of the human race. We have a good government, but we can, or ought, to make a better one ; if not we can prepare the road so our children may reach the goal. We must try and allay the passions, and not be controlled by their demands. Perfection is the acme of human ambition, beyond which we cannot go, but toward which we are in duty bound to climb. We must progress ; if we do not, we shall recede. We must go onward and upward till we can reach no higher. Till we reach this we must be merciful and lenient toward our vanquished brethren ; for just so long as we do not exercise these virtues, we must, as a necessary consequence, have war ; and if the course which we delight so much to pursue be the cause of war, then, in our settlement of our differences we should not be severe, revengeful, and arrogant to those whom fortune has decided against ; for we should remember that good fortune is not always with the strongest ; that the slightest event may be sufficient to change the fate of millions ; and that we may yet ourselves be reduced to the same condition. We must think now how we should like to be used in case such an event might happen, and do unto them just as we should like to have others do unto us. If we be disdainful and unrelenting to our fallen foe how shall we feel when others more humane than ourselves, choose to reward our severity with kindness ? Would we not then reproach ourselves for being too arrogant in the hour of prosperity toward our own unfortunate brethren, when strangers are merciful to us in the hour of adversity ? Would not mercy be a virtue to them, if it would be to us under like circumstances ? Then why not exercise it ? Why not make a road now while the sun shines so brightly, that we may find our way along when clouds overshadow us ? Do we presume to think that we will always be victorious and no conquerors be found to put down that overbearing spirit which too often follows in the path of success ? Let us pave the way to our own salvation. Let us do that now which we will not be ashamed to ask of others ; nor be ashamed to receive mercy when we thought our brother unworthy to receive it. Then we shall not be ashamed to accept from the hands of others that which we so freely conceded in like circumstances.

WE SHOULD BE WISE IN TIME.

We, or our successors, may yet be driven to the extremity of appealing to the sword, and we, or they may get whipped ; we cannot tell. It is well to look ahead and prepare for such an emergency. Our vanquished foes may in time regain their strength, and fortune may crown their endeavors with success. They may regain their lost power. Think of such a contingency, and tremble. Think what pleasure they would feel in being revenged on you for the indignities which you now heap on them. Perhaps that revenge would be just, because yours now is unmerited. They have done nothing to provoke such extreme measures, except to fight valiantly in defence of cherished principles ; and which you yourself would do if you deemed your rights endangered, or your liberties curtailed ; and which you would have a perfect right to do ; for we have as much right to anticipate a danger by adopting such means to prevent it as we shall think necessary, as we would have, if the danger were evident, and existing.

NEGRO SUFFRAGE.

This is not all. The party in power urge upon the Executive the necessity of not only taking away from the whites the elective franchise, but even to extend it to the negro ; thus placing the whole white population of the South in the hands of an ignorant and revengeful class. Think of four millions of these beings holding complete domination over twice their number ! A sect uneducated in any branch of civil, social, religious, and political science ! who know nothing of government, of laws, or a moral duty ! who have neither art, intelligence, or refinement ! who have never shown any remarkable degree of ingenuity, skill, or aptitude of invention ! A people, who for nearly 5,000 years have not advanced one step in the development of their mental powers ! who to-day are as sunken in all the vices of barbarism, cannibalism, infanticidism, and promiscuous concubinism as they were 3,000 years ago. Think of such a people being placed over an intelligent and patriotic one ! The mind reels with horror at the thought ; and the Christian weeps tears of sorrow when reminded of such ingratitude from man to man. He also mourns to see man so lost to a sense of those redeeming qualities which are the pride of humanity and the glory of a golden age. Talk of reason, or law, or justice to any of them, and you will be scoffed into silence. They would say, "we don't reason with traitors; the halter is the only justice." But why, some may inquire, why not let the negro vote as well as other ignorant and unread of the race? I have no objection to his voting provided only that no one other than his own race is injured thereby. I am willing he should vote all the days of his life without stint or scruple, but not at my ballot-box. I dont want a nigger's hand in my pie, nor his impudence in my business. I want the nigger to tend to his own concerns; and I believe that I can tend to mine without his help. Not that I consider myself any better than a negro, nor any other living creature, but I believe they are a class distinct by themselves and should be, like all other animals, kept in their own sphere. There is room enough on this globe for us all to live without settling down into a nigger's nest. I don't want anything to do with them whatever, and, as far as I can avoid it, I never shall. But the idea of giving them dominion over the whites is too palpably a violation of moral duty to be further considered in this place. I cannot argue it with anything like composure and resignation; and those who can conscientiously advocate such a measure show, too conclusively, into what a deplorable situation we are placed.

WHAT IS TO BE DONE WITH HIM?

But the negro is among us and is to be disposed of some way or an other; and if I had all the power requisite to carry into practical operation any measure designed to remedy the evil, I know not what course I should pursue; but I could quickly and easily determine what course I would not pursue; and that course would be opposed to their having civil, social, and political existence with the whites, for fear of the evils which would result from miscegenation. These will be treated of in their place.

But firstly, in this place, what evil will result, aside from miscegenation, if they enjoy civil, social, and political existence with us? I know of none. But there will be inconveniences and disgusting associations, which will be far from pleasant to any one concerned. Undoubtedly, such a course would be beneficial to the Africans; but it would, in the same proportion, be detrimental to the Americans. As one is advanced, the other will recede. One will rise, while the other will fall. I don't know as it would be strictly an evil to have a negro congress or a negro president, or a negro judicature; but, this I know, that it would prove that no

white man possessed sufficient confidence and influence in and on the American mind to merit the position. Such an event would be the shame of the Americans, and the glory of the negro. The latter would trample on the majesty of the former, and, if not sufficiently wise, with arrogance and contempt. It would, too, be very disagreeable not only to us, but to our children; for they must mingle with black children, in school and out of school, as we must with older ones, indoors and out of doors, and, finally, in bed and out of bed. They would have the benefit of the advance which we have made in arts and sciences, and also of that which we shall hereafter make. This mixed socialism can never result in any good to ourselves while here. I would advise such a step hereafter; for then, I suppose, distinctions in sex, color, and propensities, will be abolished; but now the line of demarcation between the two races should be plain and distinct, for reasons which I shall hereafter give.

In the first place then, if they be not worthy of social existence with us, what shall be done with them? This is the question, and it is to the point. It is obvious that they must live somewhere; but, with us, it would be disagreeable, impolitic and unwise. I would advise that they be colonized somewhere alone, where they may be left at liberty to propagate their species, and improve the arts to their hearts'-content unmolested; then no one will be brought down by their advance. The act, or law, which orders their removal and colonization should provide means for their sustentation, and implements of husbandry, and such other articles as shall be thought necessary, together with a clause prohibiting at once and forever all social intercourse with them which is not of a diplomatic or state character; and any one who infringes on this last clause to be condemned to perpetual and ignominious exile in the country of the blacks. It is believed that this would be sufficient to deter fickle or philanthropic lovers from throwing themselves into the arms of a wench, and, also, as an antidote for feminine love of the effluvia of black flowers. If I thought a descendant of mine would outrage the majesty of white blood to such an extent, I would forever live in single blessedness, preferring rather to see a race unbegot, than to see it thus disgrace its name. To be banished forever with them would take off a good deal of the romance. They would get rather more of black blood than they wanted.

As to the place where such a colony might be founded, little argument is necessary. We have land plenty on this continent for the building up of a negro empire; and it can raise itself up in emulation opposite our own. Give them New Mexico and a part of Texas, or other lands as may be thought best. There is room enough yet, plenty. There are thousands of square miles which no civilized foot has ever yet trod, and which will not be, unless some such measure be adopted, for years to come. Don't then, for the sake of them, for the sake of ourselves, and for the sake of our God, permit them to remain with us in any capacity whatever, for whether slaves or free-slaves, or by whatever other term you choose to designate them, the case is just the same, and the danger just as evident. If they can be made anything, they can make themselves just as well as for us to unmake ourselves. If they can be useful to us, they can be useful to themselves. It is not necessary that we lose ourselves in negro blood in order to rescue them from the grovels of misery and woe. Better that four millions remain black, than the whole world sink into disgrace and oblivion. Better have them always remain where they are than to pull the whole white race down to their level. If they remain amongst us, miscegenation will be the result, and we shall become a heterogeneous people, divided into a half-a-dozen different castes and grades and distinctions.

The course which these negro-philanthropists pursue is instigated by no patriotic motive; all they seek is to sustain themselves in power; and they hope, by putting the ballot into the hands of the negro. he will always exercise it as they desire; for they care no more for the negro other than to make him an instrument for the upholding of themselves. They are just as jealous of their blood and beauty as any one; but if any of the servile whites choose to mix this blood, why, they will smile upon it, and pronounce it patriotic devotedness. Some few of them may set the example, to be afterwards despised by his circle, and also by his new associates. If a man thinks so little of himself as to throw himself into such society, every one, in their secret hearts, will think as little of him. To be thought much of, a man must commence by thinking much of himself; if he cannot, he may rest assured that no one else will; and the lordly abolitionist thinks as much of himself as any one else, and is just as tenacious of his prerogatives. He would not sleep with a wench himself; and if his son should fall in love with one he would disinherit him; and if his daughter should elope with a negro she would find an inhospitable roof on her return; but if his hired man chooses to sink himself a peg or two lower, why, perhaps he will be worth just as much to him, and it will make him more dependent.

6

Negro suffrage and miscegenation are inseparable. If you give him the right to vote, and continue it, you concede with it the right of marrying into your family, however much opposed you may be to this. And if you consent that the negro have social and political relations with you, you'd at the same time consent that he marry some one of your family; for how is it possible to avoid it? Will you have a negro schoolhouse, and a negro meeting-house, and a negro burying-ground, and a negro ballot-box? Do you expect while your relations are so intimate, to keep the line drawn between the two races so broad as to preclude all passing and repassing? Impossible. You must cut them off, now and forever, if you would preserve your blood untainted. Even if you have different schoolhouses and places of worship, — and what a republic would ours be with such an arrangement of things? — still there would be danger of miscegenation. A negro might get rich; he might have an only and beautiful black daughter, who he might think should be rewarded by the hand and heart of a white man. She might have plenty of black suitors, but no white ones of the right stamp, unless she happened to be immensely rich; then a white lover of moderate pretensions might present himself. If she be an heiress of a moderate fortune, it would be useless for her to aspire to the position of a white autocrat's wife; but others, of a lower grade, might be found, who would think it more preferable sleeping with a wench who could support them in idleness sumptuously, than to marrying a poor white girl, and work out an existence by hard labor. There are many who would prefer indolence to an honest and noble poverty.

The danger is increased ten-fold by having their children and ours associate on terms of perfect equality. Improper intimacies will exist, even in youth; and these will ripen with increasing age, until yellow children, white and black children, and then children little whiter than yellow, all these mixed and remixed, till the color is finally lost in the masses. A few will, perhaps, preserve themselves uncorrupted by negro blood; and these will finally be obliged, by the overwhelming majority on the other side, to mix with the rest; so there will be no distinction, but the race will become more and more degenerate and effeminate, as we now see in the Mexicans and in the South American states. The Indians and blacks have crossed, making one caste; the whites and blacks have crossed, thus making another; the whites and Indians another; and, lastly, the Spanish, who have not mixed their blood but with their own kindred and kind. What a conglomerate condition of affairs, and how clashing their interests are. I need not here add. They revolutionize their government almost every year. Each caste, or clan, wars against another. Every one is jealous of another. Every one weighs the amount of negro blood in his veins, and fears another, — perhaps his rival, — may have less. So it will be here, if these negroes be allowed to stay with us. I wish they were back where they came from. They, perhaps, can stand it to live and die in barbarism as well as their more unfortunate brethren, though I believe it to be their good to be taken from there. Yet it is not for ours to have them in our families. Colonization is our only salvation.

Who, then, some one would probably inquire, will cultivate the cotton and rice fields? Europe is overflowing with honest, sturdy whites, who would gladly embark in agricultural pursuits, if sufficient inducements were offered them, to engage in cotton culture. They are now flocking to the West. Turn the current toward the South by giving them the same inducements there, and you will see how quick the country will be settled by a sturdy yeomanry. Of course they will not settle down in the midst of negro huts. Remove these, and thriving farm-houses will take their places. Then the country will be blessed; now it is cursed.

Americans! be patriots and do something great and magnanimous. Do it for yourselves and them, and posterity will reward you with their thanks. Do something memorable and kind. Remove these people to a settlement by themselves, and your reward will be great. Your fame will be enduring, and monuments will be raised to perpetuate your memory by a grateful posterity. It will be a blessing to them and to you forever. Though they may think it now a great hardship, yet then they will see the utility. No doubt they will advance faster under our tutorship, but not half so sure. Though they pull us down to their level, still their children will suffer in the same ratio as ours do. It will make each other more miserable. Though there may be a kind of revenge in seeing their stock engrafted on ours, still their children will deplore it as a direful catastrophe; not so much because they are part white. A child or man would regret it more for being yellow than he would for being black; for he would seem to be between, and trying to become white and cannot. Whatever is done with them I hope it will result in their good and to our glory. Let wisdom and not

faction, guide our counsels and justice will follow; and what is right is good. In dealing with this question no selfish considerations should enter our minds. We should be all in all for the country. If we desire to work for her interests our own will result; for we and our country are one. We are linked inseparably together. Thence, it may be to our apparent interest to consider ourselves, and the salvation of ourselves; but such interests are only momentary and ephemeral; there is nothing enduring and stable in them. They dazzle our eye for a moment, and are pleasant, but they soon pass away, leaving us to be mocked by their shadow.

APPEARANCES NOT REAL.

Do something self-sacrificing if you would receive laudatory praises. The people can see and determine respecting your merits. They know whether your patriotism is instigated by love of country, or by love of party. They cannot be duped by your sophistry. They can see through your devices and understand well what is your object. If left to them the question would be decided according to the strict letter of our principles. If man's interests are safer in his own hands, the people know this and they will not betray themselves. The people are the safest depositories of public trusts. If left to them the negro will have justice; though at the hands of a set of unscrupulous politicians, I believe he would be wronged.

PEACE IS PROCLAIMED.

After four years of desolating war, peace again smiles upon us. Not such a peace, however, as was once our lot, but a peace freed from the horrors of bloody strife. Even for such a peace we should be thankful, though we do not all of us partake alike of the blessings which a general cessation of arms would confer. The sword is sheathed in all our land. The cannon has ceased to belch forth its leaden hail of carnage and death. The war-horse no longer tramples on the fair, yet mutilated forms, of bleeding patriots. Our homes are no longer laid waste. Our fields are no longer made desolate; but still we do not enjoy to the full extent the blessing of that hallowed boon. Partisan contention is again active. We are too apt to condemn the acts of others without sufficient forethought. If we take a partisan or one-sided view of the issue before us, we would either heartily commend, or uncharitably censure the course which leading statesmen take. In order not to follow either of these extremes, we must examine the motives and objects, before we either applaud or reprove. Having sifted the case thoroughly in our own minds, alone in our closets, after hearing the arguments on both sides, of patriotic statesmen, and also of interested politicians, and being fully persuaded of the truth or falsity of the point in question, we should then proceed to deliver our opinion in a calm and dispassionate manner, free from all maliciousness on one side, and arrogance on the other. Neither should success make us abusive, nor defeat, servile. If we have conquered, we should be modest, and generous, and merciful; if we be defeated, we should be brave, — not asking too much, nor expecting too little. To be moderate in prosperity, and brave in adversity, are virtues which we should all of us cultivate. Yet to expect that these would all be exercised by every one, is rather more than we can ask from the frailties of human nature. We are what we are, endued with passions and propensities, and until we can bring these under the control of the will, and reason unshackled by their demands we cannot hope to solve truthfully an abstract problem, nor adjust our differences in a fraternal manner.

IS CONGRESS CENSURABLE?

Before answering this question, we must examine the motives of those interested, or those who now wield the destinies of the American Republic. We must see whether they are devoted to party, or to the country. In such a small treatise these questions cannot be fully discussed. Of course we cannot expect others to see exactly as we do. Every one has a mind, and, in this country, the right to use it: we cannot, therefore, dictate to another the course which he should pursue. He may think his course as patriotic and as disinterested as the one which we might suggest.

We will first see whether the course which Congress is pursuing is designed to further the ends of party, or advance the interests of the country. If party and country are synonymous, then all that they have done or are doing is for the interests of the country; if not then they are distinct and separate. The principal aim of Congress seems to tend to the establishment of themselves in power. If it is good for party to be in power, then all they have done is good; if not, otherwise. Is it for the good of the country that but two-thirds of the United States be represented in Congress? It is good to have liberty and independence, and the privilege to legislate for ourselves. The reverse of this

is bad; therefore it is not good for one part of the country to hold another part in subjection to its will. Then party and country are distinct. What means the exclusion of senators and representatives from Congress, if it is not for the purpose of upholding party? Congress knows that as soon as she accepts of delegates from Southern States, she disarms herself, and gives the strength which she would fain wield herself into the hands of her enemies. We must not too severely blame them for this; for selfishness is connate; and it is hard to bring us to believe that it is good to relinquish that which it is our apparent interest to retain. It would be patriotic for the present majority in Congress to put itself in the minority. History, no doubt, would applaud them for it; but the gratification of the present would not be so amply secured. Partisan animosities, and private resentments would not thus so bountifully be reeked on their enemies. The passions blind the reason of men, and they prevent them from seeing that, and doing what they might themselves even wish they could do. Reason and passion conflict; but the latter often prevails.

The present Congress may think that the course which it pursues is the best which could be adopted; but we can hardly believe it is sincere. We, of course, must judge by the acts which it has passed, and the resolutions which it has adopted; one of which is amendatory of the Constitution, basing representation on suffrage; thus endeavoring to force States into the adoption of laws which they have heretofore wisely, and, I might say, humanely rejected. How can such a resolution be construed as being for the good of the country? It cannot be, unless it be proved that to uphold party is to uphold the country. But how, it may be asked, can it be construed to be to the advantage of party to adopt such a resolution? Simply by putting into the hands of an illiterate class the ballot, which, as a matter of course, would be exercised to the advantage of the party conceding it. Even this is presumptive. Yet it would hardly be supposed that they would wield so powerful a weapon for the destruction of their friends. They could hardly be so ungenerous, and it would not be expected. Still they might, under a change of circumstances, be induced to exercise such a privilege for the interests of their immediate surrounding; and this, sooner or later, would be very likely to occur. That it would be for the interest of the country, no intelligent mind will contend; for whether they exercise the elective franchise in favor of one side or the other, it is very probable they would do so injudiciously, or at the instigation of an interested influence.

It is strange that our fathers failed to see this point. Why did they not extend the franchise to the negro? Have the people been so blind, in regard to a very important fact, during the whole existence of our commonwealth, that the best interests of the country can be advanced by giving the ballot to the hands of the negro? Strange they should have overlooked this; and what is stranger still, that it should have been only now discovered. In fact this has always been heretofore repudiated when left to the decision of the people in every State. We do but accuse the justice of this decision when we attempt to force it upon reluctant States.

Of course then such a course is against the country, if it is against the wishes of the people. Then it must be partisan, and not calculated, in any degree, to subserve the general good of the country; for it surely cannot be for the good of the country that two millions of uneducated beings participate in the legislative councils of the nation. This is why foreigners are debarred for five years the exercise of the elective franchise. It is necessary that all be initiated into the workings of our Constitution before they be allowed to assist in upholding and amending the organic law of the land. When they become sufficiently enlightened to discriminate between right and wrong, then, if they must abide with us, I should be in favor of any measure calculated to advance them in the scale of social existence. Till then let them be tutored in all the arts and sciences of civilized existence. It is not possible, and I appeal to the rational judgment of every dispassionate mind, for a nation of slaves, recently emancipated from the most cruel bondage, to rise at one step to the majesty and stateliness of manhood. Let them advance by a gradual progression upward to the acme of human hopes.

Suppose it be conceded; are they not as likely to abuse it, as to exercise it judiciously, and, perhaps, to their own disadvantage, and our ruin? Mexico has tried it, and other States and failed — shamefully failed. Where there is not sufficient intelligence and virtue in a nation for self-government, it is a mockery to give it to them. It accuses the nation of haste and precipitancy in giving that to another which cannot, and will not be appreciated.

Were England and Ireland capable of self-government two thousand years ago? Suppose it had been given them by some charitable nation, would it have been exercised to their advantage or to their hurt? In all probability it would have been the direst calamity which could have been conferred upon them. They were not prepared for the reception of such a boon. They must

first be educated up to that standard of intelligence and sobriety which will enable themselves to live in the enjoyment of constitutional blessings, before they are competent to discharge the obligations which such a constitution confers. Give to a fool independence, and to a spendthrift wealth, if you wish to see the former abused, and the latter squandered. It would be uncharitable and unfriendly. It would be baneful to their happiness, and a sure forerunner of their destruction. Were the people of the mediæval ages prepared for self-government? Would they have been grateful to the philanthropist who would have been so unwise as to have given it to them? They would have laughed at the credulity of those who presumed that they would have thanked them for their interference. They would have mocked them with derision and contempt; and shall we thus see our gift spurned, and we despised? Better retain it ourselves than see it thus wantonly wasted.

AN EXCUSE FOR CONGRESS.

From this, we conclude, that Congress is censurable; but, as I remarked before, we must be charitable to human infirmities; and the first of these is the preservation of ourselves in the enjoyment of the present life; and every means that will conduce to this end are by many deemed legitimate. We must, therefore, not accuse too severely, but remonstrate kindly with them, and try to induce them, from rational and patriotic motives, to desist from a course which can — though it would be unpleasant for the present — only bring upon themselves discomfiture and shame. It is almost like yielding up life itself for them at once to surrender the power which they wield. This is why Southern representatives are not admitted into Congress. The radicals by such an act would put themselves into the minority — almost into the position in which the South are now placed. They, instead of being in a position to wield the destinies of the republic, would be compelled to sue at the hands of others — their adversaries — what they are now prepared, though unwilling, to give.

The Bourbons of Europe, aided by interested kings, fought desperately in the maintenance of their prerogatives, in the beginning of the present century; neither can a rational mind censure them for it, however warmly he may espouse and advocate democratic institutions. He may deplore such an unhappy condition of things; but the weakness of human nature will for a moment triumph; yet reason will finally prevail.

CONGRESS AGAINST THE PRESIDENT.

It is a source of much regret to see Congress array itself in such hostile attitude against the President. We say that Congress is against the President, rather than the President against Congress. Congress was first to accept the issue; for it being last in the field it was its duty either to accept or reject the plan which was proposed. It chose to reject. The question now arises which is to lead, and which is to be subservient to the other? The answer is, neither. Our constitution is democratic, and not a clause in it can be so construed as to excuse any aggression which one may make on the other; on the contrary, one is designed as a check upon the other, for fear one or the other would acquire too much power for the good of the commonwealth. Every true democrat should watch with a jealous eye every assumption of power, or patronage, which is the same, not guarantied by the Constitution. They should be mutual, neither commanding the other. The President may advise, but he ought not to dictate what Congress should do. After laws are once made it becomes his duty faithfully to execute them. This is his duty, and it is obligatory upon him.

Congress is the sole judge of the right of members to their seats. This no one contests. They are the representatives of the people, and as such they must permit their acts to be scrutinized by those whom they serve. If they approve them then I have nothing to say. However iniquitous and unjust their acts, whether constitutional or unconstitutional, if sanctioned by the people, I would not murmur. The people can work out their own salvation; and before this august tribunal they must appear. If Congress rejects half the members which the people send there, they must hold themselves responsible at the next election. If they be returned, then they are approved, and no one ought to appeal from this decision. If the people approve the course which the President is following, then Congress is undone,—at least, this present radical Congress. They seem to entertain no fear of the result, so confident are they of being in the right.

THE DIFFERENCE BETWEEN CONGRESS AND THE PRESIDENT.

The difference between Congress and the President has not heretofore been sufficiently evident to cause any alarm to the more moderate republicans; but since the passage of the Civil Rights Bill over the veto of the President, parties begin to range themselves in distinct ranks. Men see that something must be done, and that speedily, or the country is ruined. Congress, by coming boldly forward, as she has now recently done, and declaring plainly what line of policy she intends to pursue, will cause the breach between Congress and the President to widen, and be more and more difficult to bridge over. Which is right? This every one must answer for himself, after weighing in his own mind carefully the policy of each. One may think Congress is right, and bring all his reason to support it, and think nothing can be brought against it; while another may come to an entirely different conclusion; and each will think himself a patriot, while his antagonist is wrong.

The difference between them is this: Congress wishes to admit the late rebellious States on the condition that the negroes be allowed the right of the elective franchise; and this they wish to secure by an amendment to the Constitution, thus making it the fundamental law of the land, and also to reckon in the negroes in the apportionment of representatives. The President wishes to leave these entirely with the States; as he contends that Congress has no right to legislate respecting suffrage. The States have formerly exercised this right; and Congress has never before interfered with it. Have the States lost this right? Will the people sanction this usurpation on the part of Congress? Will they sit idle and see one after another of their cherished sovereign immunities taken from them?—for this measure affects the North as well as the South. If Congress be allowed to usurp this right, it will form a dangerous precedent for the assumption of other State privileges. If the people allow them to take this right, they will go on and on till they have all State rights swallowed up in themselves. Then tyranny reigns, democracy being dead. O Americans, forbid! Let us not lose those inestimable blessings bequeathed as a legacy by our revolutionary fathers. Permit them not to usurp one after another of those rights which every true American holds dearer than life itself. Even those who now look with indifference, or perhaps side with Congress, will live to rue it in tears and blood at no very distant day. For what could a people more justly take up arms? Nothing. It caused a war between Parliament and King Charles I., and was not amicably settled until thousands of lives had been lost, and millions wasted. If a little firmness and prudence had been exercised in time, all this could have been prevented, and the country saved from the ravages of civil war. Does the American people again wish to see their country deluged in fratricidal blood? Only see what a small, and insignificant, and unnecessary beginning this is. It is the right of universal negro suffrage based on constitutional law. This has been uniformly forbidden by the intelligence and policy of the American people? Shall a knot of interested politicians force it upon the people? Shall they force us again into civil war? for it would ultimately result in civil war; as the people cannot, will not, I trust, look indifferently on and see all their most cherished rights, ravished one after another, from them; and if this point is conceded, against the wishes of the Executive, others will be asked, and forced, if necessary, from him and from the people. Can the people see the highest office in their gift humbled, and made to subserve the interests of a set of unscrupulous fanatics, who have in view no other object than the establishment of themselves in permanent power and authority? The office of President would be merely nominal, set up for the purpose of legalizing iniquitous laws, and pledged to follow and obey the rescripts of congressional despotism.

What matters it whether a million or more of untutored slaves be allowed immediately the exercise of the elective franchise, when any and every intelligent democratic mind would not be averse to granting them this boon when they become sufficiently enlightened to act with prudence? The people can see the justice of this, and the impolicy of endangering their very national existence, by extending to ungrateful beings a privilege which they are unprepared to exercise. What use would they make of it, supposing it was granted? They can neither read nor write, nor discern any theory of government, nor understand any abstract principle. It is like giving a dollar to a monkey, who would consider it more as a toy, to suspend about its neck to laugh and grin at, than as a representative of a quantity of merchandise. Show a negro a ballot, and what will he do with it, — look, laugh, turn it over; look again, laugh again, and throw it away, wondering all the while that any one should make so much ado about it. He would not even retain it as a mark for a book. You must tell him to go and put it into a box on a table, or behind a bar; and even in doing this he would make some awkward blunders, as twisting it up so as to prevent its insertion in the slit, or stub his toe and fall down, grinning all the while at the foolish play. He would be the butt of every witticism, and a laughing-stock for every fool. A wise man would look on in shame and indignation, and retire home lamenting the fallen condition of the great American name. You might as well import a million of monkeys to do your bidding at the ballot-box. Can we not vote for ourselves? Can we not govern ourselves without the co-operation of this illiterate gang? Is not a majority of one as good as a majority of a million? for, as a matter of course, they will all vote one way, or in proportion to the predominance of the influence exercised. Suppose, for instance, the contest is equal, and I, being a radical abolitionist, — God forbid, — with supreme influence and authority, come and cast my vote, is not the case decided as emphatically as it would have been if I had brought my minions and cast a million more just as I wished them to? Certainly it is. Then why not do away with this supernumerary, and do our own voting? It will only entail upon us a greater expense, with more labor to arrive at the same result. More ballots will have to be printed, which will be at our expense, with the labor of distribution, and in trying to make them understand how and what to do.

I regret that the circumstances compel us to discuss such a question at all; but every well-wisher of his country cannot look on with indifference, and say nothing. It behoves every one to remonstrate kindly with those who erroneously believe they are working for this country, pointing out the errors of their position, and the impolicy of pursuing further such a course. All should put forward every exertion in order to avert civil dissension. We should strive with the eagerness of patriots, bringing to our aid every argument, and exerting every endeavor. Let the utterances of every patriot be heard, and the services of every true lover of his country accepted.

But for what should we be so zealous? Is there fear of ruin? Yes. Will negro suffrage ruin us? Yes. Why? Because they do not know how to vote prudently, except at the suggestion of some interested politician. Then what shall we do? What will save us? Be prudent, and virtuous, and wise. If we be prudent, we will act discreetly; if virtuous, good; and, if wise, magnanimously. We will give to the negroes justice, and be prudent at the proper time. Is not the exercise of prudence necessary to the stability and perpetuation of our institutions. Certainly; for if we had not been prudent we should not now have been in the enjoyment of the greatest blessings ever bestowed on man. Then, if we be good, we will extend these same blessings to others; yes, when they are prepared to receive them. But it would not be good in us to give these to others who are not in a condition to enjoy them.

The same arguments may be used against this question which we brought against meddling in Mexican affairs. The Mexicans are unprepared for self-government; and until they become enlightened and virtuous, it would be unwise and impolitic to give it to them. Let a people acquire it for themselves, and then, they knowing the value, would preserve it.

It is the same in regard to these negroes. We went on and fought their battles, and liberated them from slavery, without their consent, and almost without their aid. This is enough for one step. Wait now and let them learn a little in their new position, then let them advance another step; then, by and by, another. In this way they will progress faster than if you forced them to take the whole stride at once. You must advance step by step with them, as the white race has done. Man cannot advance right up to the acme of human perfection at one exertion of his will. See how many thousand years have been spent in advancing us up to where we now stand. It is just so in every science. Man must advance with patience, labor, and perseverance. The boy commences in the primer, and ends in the college, through long, weary years of study and anxiety. You cannot make a boy a man in a moment; nor a woman into a man ever, however much logic and sophistry you may employ in the attempt. True, some women are better and more competent to wear breeches than some of the male species.

THE UNION.

Another argument can be adduced, to authorize the immediate restoration of the eleven rebellious States to all the rights of other States, from the fact that the Union should be inseparable and perpetual. Then receive the eleven States into Congress and make it a Union in fact. But the radicals are unwilling to do this. Why? Because it would put them in the minority. The people, I trust, do not participate in this solicitude of Congress; neither will they be duped by its sophistries. They fought for the Union, and they will fight for it again if necessary. Many of them would rally beneath the presidential banner; few, very few, will be found on the side of despotism. If this continues, as it has begun, it will result in a war between the President and Congress. If Congress is bound to rule it must be put down. The President does not wish it, neither would he accept it if it was tendered to him and secured. The President seeks not his own ease and emolument, but the good and happiness of the country; while Congress is struggling for itself. In a conflict of arms between the two, the people will side with the President; for it is

just as right and proper that they fight for him now, as for the Union then. The President is for the Union, and Congress is against it.

I would advise that if Congress should persist in the resolution of excluding the eleven States until they comply with their requisitions, to organize themselves in a congress and proceed to business. Their ordinances would be as legal as those of the present Congress, when approved by the President. The President, according to the theory of the Union, is just as much their President as he is the President of the radicals. The representatives and senators would be nearly as numerous and as respectable as the Congress of the United States in 1798. The President would not of course approve of laws which conflicted with one another. I do not see why it is not feasible. The present Congress cannot successfully oppose it, especially after it adjourns. Let one congress legislate for one part of the Union, and the radical Congress for the other; and let the Union be represented in the President until after the next presidential election; then, after counting all the votes, even from the late rebellious States, let the candidate having the highest number be acknowledged as being duly and legally elected president. Then let the whole country settle down peaceably and amicably on this decision, and return again to the terms of the old federal compact. I hope and trust that whatever is done will be for the good of the commonwealth.

ABOUT IRELAND.

We see on a distant and long oppressed island, a nation struggling for independence. They require our sympathy, and should have, if necessary, our co-operation. This, according to international law, cannot be at once conceded. But our relations with England have, by the course which she has taken towards the late rebellious States, been of a doubtful neutrality. It is a precedent for us. We can follow the same course toward England's rebellious subjects that England adopted toward ours. If policy suggested the course which England took, it is equally our own. If Ireland struggles manfully, heroically, and long, they must and shall have our assistance; for we as liberty-loving democrats cannot be indifferent spectators of brave patriots. They must prove themselves worthy of independence before we endanger ourselves by a too hasty compliance with their requests. If they can acquire, they ought to have, liberty. Let them strike, and strike vigorously, if they would have the co-operation of others.

RETROSPECT.

I may be called, from the foregoing, a Secessionist, or a Copperhead, or whatever other term the opponent may choose to designate me and the principles which I have herein before advocated. It matters not what I may be called. The truth exists, I am, what I am. By calling me names does not alter facts, nor make that odious which is not so. I have written on the subject that which appears truth to me; others may think differently, and it appear also to them to be true. I think I stand on true democratic principles, at least, I wish to stand on these as they are those on which the Constitution is based.

I maintain that man has inherent and inalienable rights; and if man has rights men have the same; therefore, man has rights both in his individual and in his collective capacity. And again; if he has rights he has a right to maintain them. He has a right to resist aggression and oppression, and he has a right to anticipate an oppression which he deems threatening and eminent, but not actual. He has a right to revolutionize and change his government; and because he does not succeed when he attempts it, this does not nullify the right. Every State in the Union would maintain the same if a power at Washington should assume unwarrantable and aggressive authority. Suppose that power should dictate to the States what men to elect to Congress, and should refuse to accept any other, and should bring the military power of the nation to enforce his injunctions. What do you think the States would do? Kindly acquiesce? No; they would rise in arms, and drive the tyrant from his throne, or perish in the attempt.

I have endeavored in this pamphlet to show that man has such rights, and to anticipate by an apology, should the States be driven to such a necessity. This may be construed into an apology for the South; it is; it is also one for the North. The North recognize it as true, and they are now sorry that necessity compelled them to nullify it. Still they do not ignore State rights. Under different circumstances they would themselves do what the South has done. It is their over zeal and love for the whole Union which has driven them on, and they trust that the importance of the issue will exonerate them from all blame. When all parties see the value and necessity of a close adhesion to the principles and union of our fathers, I believe, and am persuaded, that not only will the South be sorry that they so rashly put in jeopardy the existence of our federal compact, but all future States will forbear and endure wrongs and injuries until the last limit of moderation is passed before they appeal to the sword. Let all be actuated by such love for our common country, and sedition and strife will cease. When this time arrives, the world has then come to the ideal standard of moral perfection. War is less general than ever before, because people see more and more the folly of it. When war ceases entirely then the millennium will follow and bless the nations of the world with a universal peace. Then concord and love will reign forever.

Let no one construe from this that I would have this nation divided up into a number of petty jealous states and communities each warring against another for political supremacy. Nor do I think it advisable for every imaginary or apparent wrong to rise up overflowing with wrath and indignation and strike down the insulter. This is the resort of passionate senseless men who disregard the promptings of the monitor within; and such a course is adverse to the dignity of the man however much others may decry such a principle. Let us all stand upon our dignity and overawe the mind of an intrusive pedant by the majesty of our demeanor and the justice of our decisions. Let every man be actuated by such principles and none will dare intrude. Let every man be sovereign of himself, and, unitedly, we will be sovereigns of the world. We must first be governors of ourselves before we can govern others. I would have these States live in harmony and union forever, but they cannot so long as the selfish propensities control our better judgment; for how can the interests of all be advanced, especially when the Canadas and Mexico are acquired, and divided into states; when the territories are inhabited and annexed to the Union — when the interests of one sectional majority are considered as of mere consequence than those of the whole! They cannot. Let us live in virtue and peace.

B. T. MUNN.

SKANEATELES, Oct. 25, 1865.